ALONE

Every tree seemed to have eyes that followed their progress back through the woods to the lodge. The fog had gotten thicker and she could see only inches ahead, two steps, three toward the lodge. She struggled to stop her mind from drifting like the wisps of fog. Why was it so quiet? No birds sang, no loons called from the lake. Even their feet made no sound because the ground was so soggy.

"Don't leave me here alone. I think there are just the two of us left. We need to stay together."

A sudden quickening of her pulse made her turn. There was no one there. She was alone.

The last one left.

Other Avon Flare Books by
Barbara Steiner

The Dreamstalker
The Photographer

Coming Soon

The Photographer II: The Dark Room

NIGHT CRIES

BARBARA STEINER

AN AVON  FLARE BOOK

NIGHT CRIES is an original publication of Avon Books. This work has never before appeared in book form.

AVON BOOKS
A division of
The Hearst Corporation
1350 Avenue of the Americas
New York, New York 10019

Copyright © 1993 by Barbara Steiner
Published by arrangement with the author
Library of Congress Catalog Card Number: 92-90442
ISBN: 0-380-76990-5
RL: 4.9

First Avon Flare Printing: February 1993

AVON FLARE TRADEMARK REG. U.S. PAT. OFF. AND IN OTHER COUNTRIES, MARCA REGISTRADA, HECHO EN U.S.A.

Printed in the U.S.A.

RA 10 9 8 7 6 5 4 3 2

For my dear friend Jean Hodges,
drama teacher extraordinaire

Thank you to Jeffrey Bullock for Hank's poem.

The line on page 94 is from *The Children's Hour* by Lillian Hellman.

All other play quotations are from *Macbeth* by William Shakespeare.

CHAPTER 1

The first sound Suzanne heard as she stepped off the boat sent shivers up her spine. A single, throbbing note floated across the lake, then became a trembling wail. *Ooo, oooo, ooo, oooo, ooo, oooo, ooo, oooo.*

"Eerie, isn't it? We've disturbed them." Lucille Stubblefield put her arm around Suzanne's shoulders. "I've heard the loon's cry all my life, and the sound still gives me goose bumps."

"Is that what that is? A bird?" Suzanne Rollins took a deep breath, made a face, and tried to relax. She was a city girl and not at all ashamed of it. She was used to cars and buses humming through the wee hours, sirens screaming all night long, and garbage trucks crashing and banging at 5 A.M. Did anyone ever get used to the moaning sounds these birds were making?

Several more loons joined the chorus, their full minor tones haunting the dark waters of the northern lake.

"It sounds like some kind of evil spirit." Tamara Tate laughed and tossed her head of frizzy black curls. Long dangling earrings shaped like Celtic crosses tangled in her hair. Even on their camping

1

trip, she was wearing five rings. Two were huge turquoise designs, and one pinkie ring sparkled like a peach colored blossom. "This island is haunted."

"We'll probably all be looney tunes before the weekend is over." Willis Hayward grinned at Suzanne and picked up his duffel bag. Curly dark red hair framed a face that Suzanne could always depend on to hold a smile.

"Does Mrs. Reed always take her play casts off someplace like this before rehearsals start?"

"Yep, she does," Willis answered. "In two short days we'll be melded into the tightly knit group that Kathleen insists on. We'll be friends for life, but all certifiably crazy, I'd guess, from the looks of this place."

"Could she have found any place more primitive?" Tamara seemed reluctant to leave the boat.

"Sure." Willis grinned. "How about an unexplored island in the wilds of Canada."

"I'd have given back my part," Suzanne said.

"Yeah, I'll bet you would." Tamara tugged Suzanne's hair playfully.

Tamara was right. Suzanne would never give this part back. Playing Lady Macbeth had been one of her favorite fantasies, her first big break for a meaty role.

Although Suzanne was new at Shoreview High this year, she had been involved in theater for years. But Mrs. Reed's creative and sometimes crazy teaching techniques were different, and sometimes disconcerting. First, tryouts for the senior play didn't consist only of reading the script and performing a prepared piece. Mrs. Reed had put them into small groups and given them theater games and improvisation to do.

Suzanne had to have a make-believe argument with Tamara. Then she'd had to pretend that Willis was her husband, and she was leaving him. It had taken all her acting ability not to laugh. Willis was about six inches shorter than she, and his devilish brown eyes had teased her all during the skit. Mrs. Reed must have been satisfied, though, since she'd cast Suzanne as Lady Macbeth, the female lead.

"Kathleen has taken us a lot of places. But this is our first trip up here." June Mason balanced a small suitcase in each hand. "We spent spring break last year in that old farmhouse she and her husband live in. It was creepy and full of spiders. This may be worse." She glanced around.

"Yeah, tarantulas triple their normal size." Willis made his hand into a spider and dangled it over June's nose.

"Willis, stop it!" June begged and stepped onto the dock.

Suzanne's first impression—after she got over the strange calls that echoed around them—was that Thunder Island was isolated, but beautiful. Heavily forested, the island was ablaze with fall color. Red, yellow, rust, and maroon leaves contrasted with the evergreens that would stay the same emerald all winter. She couldn't see any cabins or the main buildings of Sandy Point Camp, but she assumed that if they followed the winding path they'd find them.

Kathleen Reed, head of the drama department at Shoreview High School, had been the first to leap off the large boat that had ferried them from the mainland. The boat that would leave and pick them up again Sunday afternoon. Kathleen started walking uphill past an old boat house, and most of the cast were close behind her.

Suzanne was the last one off the boat, and still she hung back. Something deep inside her made her want to stay put and return to the mainland. She made a pretense of getting all her gear together and balanced in her arms.

"Feeling a bit reluctant to do this?" Tamara turned around, waiting for Suzanne.

"I guess so. How'd you know?" Suzanne was grateful for Tamara's empathy.

"I came in new last year. Most of these people have been together since grade school." Tamara grabbed Suzanne's camera before she could drop it. "I'll carry this. But you won't need a camera to remember this weekend. It'll be the highlight of the fall."

"More so than being in the play? I've dreamed of playing Lady Macbeth since eighth grade."

"Probably. It's always amazing to me how some of us feel awkward and shy about our acting, some angry because we didn't get the part we wanted, and some scared to pieces. But by the time Kathleen gets through with us, we'll be relaxed and natural in our parts and bonded forever."

"You think anyone is angry at me for getting the lead?" Suzanne asked, knowing the answer already.

"Are you kidding? Monica McCheever is furious. She's had most of the leads in this crowd since grade school. She expected to get your part, and not only because it's so juicy."

"Because of Sol getting the male lead, and she just might enjoy playing opposite him?"

4

"You get an A+ for being observant, ditto for talent, and a triple A for guts. You've made a place for yourself in this closed crowd a lot faster than I did last year. And no one could call me shy by any stretch of the imagination."

Suzanne thought Tamara lovely in a wild, gypsy way, and certainly not the least bit timid. "Remember that I grew up in New York City, Tam. We have a reputation for being aggressive. I wanted that part."

"Kathleen is very fair. You earned it legitimately. She probably preferred your low, husky voice to Monica's, too."

Suzanne and Tamara banged together more than once with all the junk Suzanne was trying to keep track of, but they walked close so they could talk.

"Want to hear some gossip?" Tamara whispered.

Before Suzanne could say, Sure, Sol Parker, who had dumped his gear, was coming back down the steep path.

"Lady Suzanne." He bowed, dark curly hair falling over his face. His long, sensitive face was that of an ascetic, but Suzanne suspected he didn't have the personality to match. "When will you learn to travel light?"

Suzanne was surprised at how glad she was that Sol returned to help them. "I was under the impression that queens would have attendants. I don't have any more than anyone else. My brother took the big suitcases to college this fall."

"And you were left with ten little ones?" Sol took Suzanne's orange duffel bag and her overnight case.

"Well, some people have to study." Suzanne shifted her heavy book bag to her other shoulder.

5

"I can't get through school on looks like you probably do." She flirted shamelessly.

"I love it," Tamara squealed. "Two months, and she has you all figured out, Solomon Grundy."

"Born on Sunday, got spoiled on Monday." Suzanne knew the nursery rhyme, but she reinvented it.

"Lost his looks by Thursday, got old on Friday, died on Saturday." Tamara finished it and Suzanne laughed.

" 'Out, damned spot!' Out, I say!" quoted Suzanne. "Is this my husband's cursed blood on my hands? Even though I would be queen and all powerful, I would wash my hands of his death."

Sol laughed at the teasing, loving every minute of it. "There are no bloody spots on the floor, but I did sacrifice greatly to let you have the best room." He led them to the back of the lodge and bounced up the steps. Turning left, he deposited Suzanne's gear on a bed, its faded plaid spread suggesting millions of washings.

"Oh." Suzanne caught her breath when she'd dumped her own load. Feeling uncomfortable so close to Sol, she hurried to the picture window.

It overlooked the lake, where the sun was setting fast. The clouds were gold and silver and blue edged. Rays like spotlights backlit the puffy curtains of mist.

"This show's for you, lady." Sol bowed dramatically as he presented the sunset to Suzanne.

"Excuse me." Tamara placed Suzanne's camera on her bed and slid into the doorway. "I'd better find out where I'm sleeping—unless we're two to a room."

"Kathleen wants us to bunk alone," Sol said.

6

"She wants us to experience the solitude, she says." His dark eyes teased Suzanne.

"Then you'd better leave." Suzanne looked up at Sol. He had the longest lashes she'd ever seen on a guy, and eyes so brown they usually looked black. His skin was even darker from a summer in the sun, but, despite his ordinary last name, she was sure his ancestors were Spanish or Aztec. Surely he had been royalty in another life.

His hand, which rested near hers on the windowsill, had long fingers, almost as exaggerated as those in an El Greco painting. She wanted to place her hand over his, but she didn't have the nerve.

His whole body was tall and lithe. Suzanne suspected he'd had dance lessons for many years. He moved with the grace and strength of a ballet star.

"Whatever you say." Sol smiled again, turned, and strode out of the room.

Suzanne had to admit she was disappointed. Was his assurance an act? She hoped to get to know him better this weekend, but she'd kept her additional agenda secret. Even Tamara didn't realize Suzanne liked Sol so much. As aggressive as she was about getting parts in plays, Suzanne moved slowly into relationships. She'd been hurt twice from being too eager and, if she wanted to admit it, too innocent. She wasn't terribly experienced at dating. She'd been too busy to get a lot of practice. Sol made her want to become experienced quickly.

Darker clouds began to swirl on the horizon, bringing the dramatic sunset to a premature close. A chilly breeze banged a shutter on the open window, reminding Suzanne she had on shorts and a tank top.

She turned to the task of unpacking. She had no idea what the weather report for the weekend suggested. But it *was* the first of October. Indian summer couldn't last forever.

Tugging on jeans and a black sweatshirt painted with two wolves, she felt much more comfortable. With some effort she shoved the peeling wooden window down, then turned again to the large expanse of glass. The clouds were now that shadowy shade of navy that suggested rain, a thunder storm. Black fir silhouettes jutted into their centers. The lake had silvered over, a still, slick mirror edged by reeds and tall grasses.

Piercing the mirror came a long, slender black neck, then a swanlike shape. Concentric circles started at the loon, moving farther and farther toward shore until they turned into choppy waves which left the grasses slightly undulating.

Just as Suzanne started to smile at the loon's center stage appearance—the show-off—she felt an even colder draft swirl through her open door.

A line from the play filled her mind unbidden.

> *By the pricking of my thumbs,*
> *Something wicked this way comes . . .*

She shook her hands, hating her wealthy imagination at that moment. But she couldn't escape the tingling that rushed into her blood and all along the veined rivers until it reached her brain.

And she couldn't shut out a repeat of the loon's chorus. This time, however, there was an urgency in the wailing, like an excited warning. The lone loon paddled across the lake's surface as if pur-

8

sued by some invisible enemy, all the while keening in a trembling voice.

Suddenly Suzanne felt afraid, unreasonably terrified.

CHAPTER 2

"Hey, Suzanne, going to look at the view forever?" Tamara came back into the room. "Where's Sol? I left you two alone for a reason."

Suzanne shook off her fear, laughing at herself. "Certainly not here."

"He likes you."

"Are you sure? He has a funny way of showing it. Well, I take that back. He seems to like me, but he hasn't done anything about it." Suzanne grinned, telling Tamara her secret by her action and words.

"He doesn't date much. He's probably deathly afraid of women, but he hates to let any of them know that. It's not macho to fear females. Come on, Kathleen wants to see all of us in the main meeting room before dinner."

"Hey, wait. What about that piece of gossip you were going to share?" Suzanne reminded Tamara. "Does it concern me?"

"Only indirectly." Tamara lowered her voice even though they were still in Suzanne's room. "Monica's mother stormed into the school an hour after the cast was announced. Summoned by her

10

spoiled little girl, of course." Tamara mimicked Monica's high voice, imaginary telephone to her ear. "Mommy, Mommy, come help me."

"Mrs. McCheever came to the school?"

"PDQ. She backed Kathleen into her office and closed the door, not knowing Bitsy Wrenn was in the closet sorting costumes. After about thirty seconds Bitsy didn't dare move or reveal her hiding place. She didn't want to get her head bitten off."

"So what did Mrs. McCheever want?"

"She wanted what rightly belonged to her baby, of course. Female lead in the senior play. She even went so far as to tell Kathleen if she didn't switch your parts, she'd get Kathleen fired."

"Could she do that?" Suzanne couldn't believe the story. She would have died of embarrassment if her mother had done such a thing. Quite often there were hard feelings after parts were given out, but most people were good sports. They got over bruised egos and settled in to work as a team. Those who couldn't do that at her old school didn't last in the theater department.

"I don't think she could, but she marched down to the principal's office once she'd found Kathleen wasn't going to budge. Then Kathleen was called in for a conference. Bitsy didn't hear that, of course."

"I still have the part, and Monica's here. She settled for being one of the witches."

"And you haven't gotten any dirty looks?"

"I didn't say that. But Monica hasn't been friendly to me anyway. I'm used to jealousy and hard feelings. We had two prima donna guys in our drama department at my old school. And re-

11

member, I've been doing theater since I was eight."

"Lucky you. You can probably make a career of it if you want to, Suzanne. You're the most talented actress I've ever seen, but then I went to a real podunk school before we moved to Minneapolis. I played a lot of leads I would never have gotten here."

"You got first witch over Monica. That's the second best female part. Let's face it, *Macbeth* is a man's play."

"Kathleen admits she chose it because she's never had so many talented senior men."

"Don't forget handsome—and even Willis is cute. Too bad she brought only the leads or we could have been surrounded by men this weekend. Come on, let's get the meeting over with. I'm starving." Suzanne hooked her arm into Tamara's, and they headed down the hall.

Suzanne didn't know when she'd made friends with anyone as quickly as she had with Tamara. They'd hit if off immediately from the minute Suzanne asked her for directions to the office. And luckily, they shared almost all the same senior classes.

"I'm sure glad you're here this weekend, Tamara," Suzanne said. "I need your moral support. Not to mention company in this place. I'll bet this lodge has been here since early pioneer days."

"Well, I don't think it's that old. I think it started as a Scout camp, but now it's privately owned and anyone can rent it."

"You think any other groups are here this weekend? You know, screaming kids or touchy-feely,

12

self-help workshops that encourage adults to risk relationships?" Something made Suzanne hope there would be tons of other people on the island.

"I've heard that people from New York City can't live without their crowds. You're weird, Suze."

Tamara had a way of reading her mind, or of filling in the blanks around what Suzanne said. It didn't bother Suzanne. Instead, it made Tamara easy to talk with. She didn't have to rattle on and on for Tamara to understand, to be on the same wavelength.

"Speak for yourself, Tamara. Sometimes I find the way you can read people a bit spooky."

"You don't know the half of it, friend. When I'm absolutely sure I can trust you, I'll tell you more about my weirdness."

"Oh no, more?" Suzanne pushed Tamara away and ran ahead of her. The pair entered the lodge's main room laughing.

"How long does it take to walk down the hall and get someone, Tamara? I may have to separate you two." Kathleen smiled when they entered, the last of the play cast to gather.

Suzanne sank onto a couch that was so soft she wasn't sure she'd be able to get out of its soft grip. Bitsy and June perched on the edge of the other cushions. Tamara melted onto the floor and leaned back, brushing Suzanne's legs.

Bitsy Wrenn asked the question Suzanne wanted answered. "Are we the only ones on the island, Kathleen?"

"I think so, except for the caretaker. Does that bother you?" Kathleen Reed had placed a straight-backed chair in the informal circle the group of drama students had formed.

"A little," Bitsy admitted. "It's sure quiet here—except for those strange birds screaming."

Bitsy was a rather strange bird herself. Not a loon, but a little brown sparrow, or wren, matching her name. And she wasn't nicknamed Bitsy by accident. She didn't even stand over five feet tall, and she had the softest speaking voice Suzanne had ever heard. She could project, though. Suzanne had been amazed during tryouts when Bitsy had become a witch. Shrieking and whining, she left the gentle bird behind and became a peacock or a fighting rooster. She had the wig she'd wear in the production to terrorize everyone. It lay beside her now, as if she was afraid she'd loose it. Against the cream-colored corduroy of the couch, it looked like a mass of hopelessly tangled, coarsely spun cobwebs.

"The loons give me the creeps." June finally relaxed into the other end of the couch.

"Everything gives you the creeps, June bug." Monica laughed, teasing June.

A short, plump girl, June Mason was good-natured and laughed a lot. Most of the time. It was also during tryouts that she revealed another side of her personality. Someone—everyone knew who—turned loose a tarantula on stage behind her. When June spotted it, her scream reached the back of the auditorium with split-second timing. At the time, Willis had whispered to Suzanne that June was terrified of insects, and especially terrified of spiders.

"We'll liven up the camp," suggested Kathleen, gathering some notes from her briefcase. "Those

14

of you who have been on our retreats before know what to expect from this weekend. But let me remind you, we're out here to bond as a group, a team. We'll be doing a lot of exercises that are designed to help you relate to each other. I also want you to be a family, a close, loving family, who are going to work together, and do whatever it takes to make this year's senior play a success."

Sol glanced at Suzanne when Kathleen mentioned loving family. He held her eyes with his, neither smiling nor revealing any feelings. It was almost as if he was studying her, waiting for her to react. To make the first move that assured him she liked him, too. Finally she released him with a smile, looking down at her hands, hoping she wasn't blushing, knowing she was.

When she looked up, it was into the green eyes of Monica McCheever. There was certainly no love lost between the two of them, and Suzanne didn't know how she was going to relate to Monica as loving family. Monica had surely seen Sol look at her. Suzanne knew the type. Monica needed to be the center of attention full-time. This trait had probably been the reason she'd joined the drama department. And she was a good actress— Suzanne would give her that. But the type that would always be hard to work with. She had argued with Kathleen about interpreting some of the female parts, even during tryouts. Some directors would have refused to work with such a temperamental actress. But Kathleen had a reputation for giving people second and even third chances if the end result was a great performance.

"Before we do anything else, I want to say

is way to write a bad re-
took him out." Everyone
y, speaking of reviewers,
One reviewer wrote this.
ame—played the role of
se was going to play the
said the actor was really
oo good a line to waste.
, though, and the remark
"
" June said.

6

Kathleen kept talking as if she wanted every bad thing she knew of to be out in the open. "Many actors's careers started downhill after they played Macbeth, and others have said their worst performances came in this play."

"We can do that," June said, and everyone agreed with a smile.

"You'd better not even consider it." Kathleen looked at her notebook. "I guess the best known fact is that Lincoln read the play the day before he was assassinated."

"Coincidence," Sol said. "We're not worried, are we guys?"

Willis frowned and quickly took the classic pose of Rodin's statue, *The Thinker*. "I want to think about it."

Mr. Wilkins, one of the senior class sponsors, had a comment. "I read that when Olivier did this role, the tip of his sword broke off and struck a member of the audience. The man had a heart attack."

Willis clutched his chest. With a loud, "ahhh," he folded up onto the floor.

Kathleen smiled and shook her head. "Lots of actors won't even call it *Macbeth*. They call it 'The Scottish Play.' Orson Welles went so far as to do a voodoo ritual during rehearsals for his version."

"That sounds like fun." June wiggled deeper into her seat.

Willis came back to life and jumped up, grabbing Monica. "Voo-doo vat you do, and I'll do zee same." He sang and spun Monica into an Astaire and Rogers movie-style dance scene. She laughed and moved gracefully with him.

17

"Okay, okay." Kathleen gave up. "I just wanted you to know many consider the play unlucky. I can see you're not going to worry or take me seriously. So now, we're going to begin with each person writing down and then sharing his or her goals." Kathleen started the first activity of the weekend.

After some exaggerated groans and grumbles, Willis raised his hand. "I can be serious, but my goal is to have fun. Are we having any fun yet, guys? Is it all right to say you just want to have fun?" He looked over his horn-rimmed glasses at the group with feigned seriousness.

"Willis, could any of us stop you from having fun?" Kathleen sighed. "It would be like stopping you from breathing. You have my permission to have a good time. I hope we'll all enjoy this. No sense doing it if we don't."

"The play or this weekend?" Hank Hopkins finally spoke up. He was the quietest guy Suzanne had ever met. She didn't think he was shy, though. He was just one of those people who had little to say. Tamara had told her that he was *the* star basketball player at Shoreview High, probably the most talented athlete the school had ever seen.

"Both, please. Now write." Kathleen studied her notebook.

"Hank doesn't say much," whispered Bitsy to Suzanne. "But you should read the poetry he writes. He's had several pieces published."

Suzanne felt her eyes widen in surprise. Not your average jock, she concluded, trying to get everyone's personality figured out. She had met all the cast, but had spent very little time with any of them except Tamara.

18

Suzanne liked trying to understand people. She treated people the way she approached a new acting role. She liked to get inside their skins and try to see life through their eyes. She kept thinking that Monica must be unhappy, but so far she hadn't tried very hard to understand her. Probably she could never come to like Monica, but stranger things have happened, she knew. She made a mental note of that for a weekend goal, too, but she wouldn't share it.

"Do you want us to play your games, Kathleen, or can Clyde and I start dinner?" The tall, elderly woman who had identified the loons for Suzanne stood up and moved toward the fireplace. Lucille Stubblefield was the other senior class sponsor who had agreed to help chaperon the weekend.

Clyde Wilkins touched a match to the fire he'd been laying while they gathered in the big room. Standing back, he watched the snap and roar of the dry kindling and newspaper with satisfaction.

"Can you trust those two alone in the kitchen, Kathleen?" Sol asked with a frown. He caught Mr. Wilkins's eye, and Wilkins gave him a thumbs-up and a big grin.

Willis added. "Yeah, who came up here to chaperon who?"

It was a well-known fact that Lucille Stubblefield and Clyde Wilkins were an item at Shoreview High. But also that they had been an item for some fifteen years. Both were near retirement. Suzanne thought it would be terribly romantic for them to run off together as soon as they stopped teaching.

Her own mother had remarried last year at forty-one. That was what had brought them to

19

Minnesota from New York City. Burt had inherited a small property on the outskirts of Minneapolis. He and her mother were going to board, breed, and train quarter horses. Suzanne had to admit she was surprised to find that her mother had always wanted to raise horses. A fashion model, who had kept working successfully, the secret desire had stayed buried until she'd met Burt Swensen.

So everyone had surprises inside, Suzanne concluded. She looked around the room. Hank writes serious poetry? Hard to believe. Bitsy could turn into a witch easily? Tamara was keeping something about her personality secret from Suzanne?

Suzanne wondered what other secrets would surface from inside the group as a result of this weekend. And, while she had never once in her entire life been truly superstitious, the list Kathleen read stayed in her mind.

SILLY! she wrote on her paper and underlined it three times. How could something—anything— bad happen just because a bunch of people performed—performed—the Scottish Play?

CHAPTER 3

A few secrets were revealed by Kathleen's first exercise to help the group get better acquainted. Suzanne knew that most of the cast had known each other for five years, but most people kept some part of themselves private.

Kathleen Reed knew that, too. "Most of you have gone through grade school and junior high together, not to mention high school. As seniors, you probably feel there isn't anything you don't know about most of your classmates. I think you're dead wrong." Kathleen smiled at her use of the word *dead*. Leaning back, relaxing, and running both hands through short, light brown hair, she let her statement sink in.

"Okay, who's been lying to us since childhood?" Willis looked around, pointing a finger at each in turn. From someplace in the khaki colored duster he wore, he'd pulled a Groucho Marx nose with glasses. He pursed his lips under the fuzzy caterpillar-like mustache that completed the look.

Laughing, Kathleen finished explaining her assignment. "One of the most important themes in the story of *Macbeth* is the idea—fact, probably—of there being something evil inherent in each of us.

Were we sorely tempted to want power, glory, or greater success, we'd not hesitate to dip into this darkness. The other theme is the tendency of power to corrupt."

"Can't lack of power also corrupt?" Sol asked.

"Yes, certainly if a person is driven to get power, control, by whatever means it takes."

"In other words," Tamara added, "a person will do anything to get power." She wasn't asking, but making a statement.

"Yes, by dipping into that evil. I want each of you in turn to give us an impromptu speech on that darkness within you. Please don't tell me it isn't there." She held up her hand as several started to protest. "You may not even be aware of it. You may not want to acknowledge it, but it is there, believe me. And should you want something badly enough, you'd use it."

"Can we make up something?" asked June.

"I might have known, June bug, that you'd think you were too goody-goody to have an evil self," Monica teased.

Kathleen ignored Monica. "If you have to, June, invent something. Be creative, but make us believe you." Kathleen smiled an almost evil smile. She knew the assignment would upset people. "Suzanne, you're new here. You start."

Suzanne thought fast. *Why me?* She let the first thing that came to her mind prompt her talk. "I'm afraid of being alone—I mean all alone. I can be alone in my room at home, or go for a walk, that sort of thing. But I guess I'd do anything to keep from being really alone, like—like being lost in the woods, or the last survivor of a shipwreck or holocaust, or—or . . ." She was running out of

22

words. She rambled on about being born in a city where you could be alone among millions of people, but they were still visible, and that her fear probably came from this environment.

Everyone looked to Kathleen for some comment when Suzanne stopped talking. She made none, which for some reason made Suzanne feel even more foolish for sharing her secret. And angry. She felt unreasonably angry when Kathleen moved the focus immediately to June Mason. "June, what about you?"

June talked about her fear of insects and where it might have come from. She mentioned past lives and phobias.

"You're getting sidetracked. This isn't what you're afraid of, although you may be afraid of this dark side," Kathleen reminded them. "This can be something you cultivate, something you have accepted as there, inside, even if it scares you."

Hank surprised everyone by volunteering. "I'm fascinated by death. The process of death, dying, what happens afterwards. How each of us will face death. I've collected death scenes from Shakespeare and other literature, death speeches, death scenes from movies. I'm fascinated by the fact that most of us fear death, even though it's a natural process, a part of life."

"And most of your poetry is about death," Bitsy added.

"Would you go so far as to kill someone to study his or her reaction to dying?" asked Sol. "Or to get something you wanted?"

"I can't say that I wouldn't." Hank smiled a rare

smile. "But I don't think I'm that obsessed by this interest."

When what was supposed to be a speech turned into a dialogue, Kathleen let it continue. Maybe this was what she wanted to achieve in the first place, Suzanne thought.

"I've heard you have to sleep with someone to get a great part in Hollywood, but I'm not sure I'd kill to get a break." Monica grinned. "But if I have to murder someone, I'll call and let you watch, Hank."

"Thanks, Monica." Hank finished talking with a sleepy smile.

"I've heard that comics are really moody, insecure people. They're hiding a Woody Allen–type angst." Willis took off his disguise and slipped it into a large pocket. "I'd probably have to admit I started being funny when my parents divorced. No one paid any attention to me, so I learned how to get people to laugh. I really wanted to cry all the time. And I think I hated both my parents."

"Do you still hate them?" asked Kathleen.

"I—I don't think so."

This was the first time Suzanne had heard Willis say anything real, anything serious, since she'd met him. She knew he was taking a risk to share this.

"I think there's still a dark, lonely place deep inside me, and I'd kill for a few good jokes to make me laugh, to make other people laugh." He switched back to his joking manner. "Did you hear this joke about three guys who had to tell Saint Peter the truth about the worst thing they'd done on earth—"

24

"Your minute is up, Willis," Kathleen interrupted. "You can tell jokes at dinner."

Bitsy confessed next, saying she had a big ball of anger inside her that she'd had to learn to live with, not to mention control. She didn't know where it came from. Monica tagged right onto Bitsy's talk and said she did, too. The two had a dialogue about anger, which Kathleen let go on until it included everyone.

Two interruptions ended the discussion and the exercise.

"Dinner in fifteen minutes," Clyde Wilkins announced, coming from the kitchen. "Those who were supposed to help cook tonight can clean up instead."

From behind Mr. Wilkins came two men with armloads of wood. They headed for the fireplace.

"Are you Mr. Russell, the caretaker?" Kathleen stood, but indicated that no one was to leave. "We'd like to meet you and your son."

The man who turned had a wild look about him. His faded red hair was long, held back by a leather thong. The lower half of his face was covered with a beard and mustache which ran together. It didn't hide his scowl, however, and maybe some surprise at being spoken to.

"I'm Russell. If you need anything, you can call the number listed by the kitchen phone."

Kathleen looked a bit disconcerted. "And—and your son?"

"My son don't talk to no one." Russell dumped his load of wood in the box beside the fireplace with a crash.

The young man, who was probably fourteen or fifteen, looked frightened, perhaps reading his father's mood. He did glance at the gathering of students, but seemed ready to run. His blue eyes, deep seated in a face that was all sharp angles, darted about the room. There were dark smudges under his eyes and on his cheeks, suggesting that he wasn't well. His eyes stopped at Suzanne's for just a second, then darted away.

Suzanne was reminded of a friend who had become anorexic, whose bones began to show all over her body before she was hospitalized. Her eyes held that same lost, lonely look.

Kathleen didn't try to get Mr. Russell to talk any more. She turned her attention back to her students. "Okay, people, take a ten-minute break, then we'll eat in the kitchen. I checked it out earlier. It's really homey."

"Dinner." Willis clutched his stomach and pretended to feel faint. "At last we can have fun eating dinner."

"Need someone to walk you to your room?" Sol took Suzanne's arm. "I'm glad you confessed that you never like to be left alone. Maybe I can help with that."

"Maybe you can." Suzanne flirted, needing company right then. Despite the roaring fire, which had heated the big room nicely, she felt cold, shivery. It had probably resulted from the caretaker and his obvious message to leave him and his son alone. They must have some reason to live on this island year-round. If they wanted solitude they got it most of the time. Maybe they hated people even coming onto the island.

Sol left her at her door. "Bathrooms and showers are down this hall." He indicated a hallway that ran along the back of the lodge. "My room is right next

26

to yours. I can hear you yell if you get a loneliness attack."

"Day or night?" She flirted further.

Shrugging, Sol smiled, turned, and left.

"Don't make a fool of yourself," Suzanne whispered into her suitcase. She dug out a red-and-black-checked wool jacket. She had picked it out because it looked like a Minnesota style. But red was a good color for her, setting off her pale blond coloring. She freckled instead of tanning, so she didn't spend a lot of time in the sun.

A full moon slid up the sky, throwing a ribbon of silver across the lake. Feeling snug and warm in the jacket, Suzanne stepped out onto the back porch of the lodge to drink in the scene. Appreciation of nature was new to her. She hardly ever saw the sun rise or set in New York City, and the moon appeared from behind some building long after coming over the horizon.

Backlighting the jagged line of spruce, the natural spotlight featured several loons. One by one, as if on cue, they sailed from behind a scrim of patchy fog, rising from the ebony water.

Next came the expected wail, not unlike the cry of a wolf or a coyote. Suzanne had heard wolves only in movies, but it was the only comparison she had for the loon's voice.

"The Cree Indians called it the cry of a dead warrior forbidden entry into heaven," said a voice behind Suzanne.

"Oh!" She jumped, then realized it was Hank.

"Sorry if I frightened you. It's beautiful, isn't it?"

"*Eerie* is a better word. I keep wanting them to

call out again, and every time they do, it frightens me."

"Look carefully and you can see his neck stretched out as he calls." Hank pointed to a single loon, now seemingly alone since the others had disappeared.

Suzanne strained to see the bird in silhouette as the high, resonant single tone faded at the end to a lower register.

"It's so similar to the call of a wolf," she said.

"Not really. It's far too ghostly, too detached from the earth. The Chippewa Indians believed the loon's cry was an augury of death."

"Hank, please." Suzanne laughed nervously and hugged herself, starting to feel the chill of the night air combined with the wailing, now a duet. "Where did you hear that?"

"I've read about them. They fascinate me. They usually only wail in duet at night. No one knows why."

"Maybe they get lonely."

"Animals don't get lonely."

"How do you know? I don't think we should judge what animals feel or don't feel."

"Have it your own way." Hank laughed softly. "Listen. If you want to give your imagination free rein, and give him human emotions, you could say he's laughing at us. Or that it's the laugh of the deeply insane."

The fluttery warble that echoed through the darkness could be compared to laughter, Suzanne thought. Insane laughter. She wanted to laugh right then to break the spell Hank was weaving around them. She really didn't want any part of his obsession with death. And the idea that the loon's call foretold death wasn't a thought she wanted to entertain for long.

She didn't get a chance to laugh at Hank to break his poetic spell. Before she could accuse him of being melodramatic, before she could say, let's go eat dinner, enough of this conversation, someone interrupted for her.

A scream overlaid the loon's next mournful cry. It was no bird's call, but that of a terrified woman.

CHAPTER 4

Suzanne was frozen in place for a moment, then she dashed inside, Hank right behind her. The scream had come from down the hall, and echoes lingered to lead them to June's room.

The first thing that Suzanne focused on was June, backed into one of the tiers of bunk beds. Her face was contorted, blue eyes were wide with fear, and the back of her hand was pressed to her mouth.

Following her eyes, Suzanne looked at June's bed, a lower bunk. It was covered with spiders of all sizes. Granddaddy longlegs, wolf spiders, small green spiders, large gray spiders. All were harmless, as far as Suzanne's knowledge went, but the sight of so many together, crawling, crouching, waiting, sent a shiver through her own stomach. She couldn't imagine how June felt, with her phobia of them.

"Who—" Suzanne started to ask.

"Gotcha!" Monica tumbled into the room, squealing with demonic glee. "Willis and I have been collecting and saving them for days. Our patience paid off, June bug. Some scream."

"Monica, how could you?" Suzanne moved to

30

June and put her arms around her. June huddled, face in her shoulder, like a small child. She was sobbing now and couldn't stop.

A grin spread over Hank's face. He shook his head over and over. Everyone was gathering, but no one seemed angry, or even dismayed, except June.

"What's the matter with you guys?" Anger filled Suzanne, and she made no attempt to hide it. "This isn't funny. How could you do such a thing, Monica? Or you, Willis? It's cruel."

"Easy," Monica said. "She's such a baby. Not one of those spiders would hurt anything except a fly, Junie. You've got to get over jumping and screaming every time you see one."

"How can you decide what fears someone else needs to get over?" Suzanne was ready to punch Monica. "A little sympathy might help."

"Oh, Monica does this all the time, Suze," said Hank. "She's a biology freak. Don't get your dander up. June should be used to it." He turned and left the room.

"Right on, Monica. Now we're having fun." Willis applauded. He and Monica bowed.

Kathleen had apparently been watching and listening. "Suzanne is right, Monica. It's not up to you to cure June of her fears. You and Willis gather up every one of those spiders and take them outside. I'll talk to you later. Right now, I think we all need something to eat."

No one said much when they gathered in the big kitchen to load their plates with food they'd all brought from home. But every time Suzanne looked at Monica, she grinned, still enjoying her

31

joke. Apparently this bunch was used to Monica's and Willis's practical jokes. Did they play them on everyone or just June?

Willis answered part of the question. "Now I know who put a frozen frog in my lunch last week. Tasty little hummer." He licked his lips and smacked them, taking a big bite of fried chicken.

"If June wouldn't carry on so, Monica would stop bugging her." Bitsy sat down between Suzanne and Willis.

"Stop bugging her? I can't believe you said that." Willis pinched his nose. "Terrible joke."

Bitsy giggled. "It was an accident."

"Even worse, then, Bits. Besides, I'm the comic in this crowd."

Suzanne still didn't think any of them were funny. She watched as Sol slid into place beside June. He leaned over and hugged her, and she tried to smile. Her eyes were red, her nose shiny. Suzanne liked Sol for caring. It seemed that no one else did. She wasn't even sure that Kathleen was bothered by Monica's and Willis's behavior.

"I was going to save the bonfire for tomorrow night, but nobody's saying we can't have two fireside meetings. As soon as we do dishes, let's all go down to the beach," Kathleen suggested.

"Should we look for some wood?" Hank asked. "We can take some of the fireplace wood."

"I called Mr. Russell to take some down." Kathleen gathered her dishes, still sipping her coffee. "Tonight's fire will be ready to light."

The moon made it almost light enough to get down the path to the lake without a flashlight. The group grew unusually quiet. Even the loon hadn't called to them.

Sol touched off the pile of kindling, adding some short logs as soon as it began to snap and pop.

Suzanne stared at the flames, releasing some of the anger she still had stored up for Monica. June was sitting by her, so maybe Monica had apologized. Suzanne had seen them together in the hall at school many times. It appeared they were friends, despite the way Monica acted. June was like an abused woman who kept returning for more. Suzanne had read about the syndrome, and she always wondered why any woman would continue to seek abuse.

She found she had to continually remind herself not to say too much or to try to change people's habits. She was wise enough to know if this crowd had hung out together for years, it had changed the group dynamics when she had come in. She and Monica would never be friends, she knew. But most of the group accepted Suzanne like they had Tamara a year ago.

Most of the time, Monica ignored her. If Monica liked Sol, she wouldn't appreciate Suzanne moving in on her territory—or, for that matter, Sol acting as if he was attracted to her. That would threaten Monica, Suzanne was sure. She certainly didn't want to be the object of any of Monica's practical jokes, so she'd move slowly.

Willis's jokes seemed to be mostly verbal. She could handle that and give it back. Suzanne wondered if he and Monica teamed up often. She hoped not.

Sol had folded his long legs to sit beside Suzanne.

His knee touched hers slightly. She was very aware of his presence and glad he was there. To her surprise, Hank had his arm around Monica, whispering to her. She nodded and smiled at whatever it was he was saying. Don't try to figure all these people out, Suzanne told herself. Just enjoy whatever happens next.

"What secret part of our souls are we going to share tonight, Kathleen?" Willis asked, breaking the silence.

"Lucille and I have no secrets." Clyde had his arm around Miss Stubblefield. "Right?"

"Shut up, old man." Miss Stubblefield frowned at him.

Kathleen laughed. "Let's rest and tell ghost stories."

"Oh boy, Girl Scout camp." Willis poked at the fire.

"And how would you know anything about Girl Scout camp, Mr. Laurel and Hardy?" asked Tamara.

"I've got a kid sister. Fess up, Tam. I'll bet you were never in Scouts or Camp Fire Girls, were you?"

"What makes you say that?" Tamara acted as if Willis had hit a sore spot.

He laughed. "Just guessing. Just guessing."

"There's a ghost in *Macbeth,*" Kathleen reminded them, "So we're not really abandoning the play. I'll start a story and pass it on. Each person has to add to it." She stared at the fire for a minute. "*Rumor has it that the camp on the island is haunted, but no one has ever seen the spirit. By tradition, she wanders only during the small hours*

34

of the night when most are sleeping. But one night, when Catherine couldn't sleep, she walked down to the lake. It was then she heard the cry for help."

The loon timed its call perfectly. His haunting cry echoed across the lake. They all laughed, but the sound had made Kathleen's story so real. And Suzanne realized she'd been waiting for the sonorous moan.

Shivering and hugging herself, Suzanne took up the tale. *"At first Catherine thought the sound was that of the loons who lived on the lake. But after the first shriek, the voice dropped to a whisper calling her name. 'Catherine. Catherine. Come. Come.' Fog fingers beckoned from the middle of the lake. 'Come,' Catherine, come to me.' "*

"She tried to resist." Sol continued when Suzanne looked at him and indicated it was his turn. *"But the invitation tugged at her heart like that of the sirens pleading to seamen to rescue them. Like someone sleepwalking, she approached the water."*

At that place in the story, Suzanne spotted the boy, the caretaker's son. He hadn't meant anyone to see him, but he had crept close to the fire and crouched by a tree listening. Her first impulse was to motion for him to join them, but maybe it would spoil his fun. He would probably run. Was he lonely out here with only his father's company? He seemed to be near their age. Did he go to some school? Had he ever gone to school?

She lost track of the middle of the story, but now Hank had Catherine sinking into the lake, only the tips of her fingers showing.

It was up to Monica to finish the story. *"There is a whole community of dead living in the lake.*

But only a few are privileged to be called to join them. Catherine was one of the chosen. And it will be her place to make the next selection. One dark night, when she has made her decision, she will call to someone. And that person won't be able to refuse, indeed, won't want to refuse since in the lake is a place where no one is ever hurt, no one is ever lonely or abused, where there is no pain or remorse. There is only that reassuring knowledge that one was wanted, was needed, was invited to join them."

"Wow." After a few seconds, Kathleen breathed out the word softly. "Wow."

Lightning split the distant sky, and a low rumble of thunder followed. The fire was down to embers.

"Suzanne, Suzanne," Willis whispered. "Tamara, Tamara, I want you both."

Willis's joke broke the spell. Laughing, they jumped to their feet and chased each other to the lodge, leaving the adults to put out the fire and follow.

Sol had caught Suzanne and held her hand, slowing her to walk beside him. "Suzanne," he whispered, brushing the back of her neck with his lips.

His touch made her shiver and laugh. She scrunched up her shoulders and pulled away. But she hoped he wouldn't let her go.

She would never know what would have happened next.

June was waiting for her near the lodge. "Will you go to my room with me, Suzanne? Please. Just until I turn on the light and look around."

"Sure, June." Suzanne glanced at Sol, but she

36

couldn't read his face in the dim light. He released her hand and waved.

June reached in and snapped on the light. The two looked around the room. Suzanne pulled back the bedspread and looked in all the covers on June's bunk. "Nothing. Why does Monica pick on you like she does, June?"

"I don't know. She always has. I guess she thinks I'm weak to be afraid of spiders. She says she hates weak people."

"Why do you put up with it? It looks to me like you two are friends."

"A habit, I guess. Our parents are friends. I've known Monica forever. She has a lot of problems at home, and she always says she's sorry."

"Does that make it all right?"

"No. Sometimes I have terrible nightmares. I have to get up and get something to eat to get them to go away."

Suzanne didn't know what else to say to June about Monica, so she lightened the conversation. "Well, just don't wander off down to the lake in the middle of the night."

June laughed. "No way. I don't want to be chosen. Good night, Suzanne. And thanks. I think I interrupted something for you."

"Doesn't matter. We'll have another time to be together." Suzanne skipped down the hall to her room, suddenly wishing the doors had locks. The lodge wasn't really haunted; Kathleen had made that up, but it was a creepy place at night.

She lay in her bed for a long time, listening to the storm get closer and closer, then crash around the building until rain poured down, pounding on the roof. Her thoughts bounced from spiders in the bed to women walking on the lake, from fire crackling to thunder booming, and finally to Sol pulling her close. She settled on the last idea to lull her to sleep.

CHAPTER 5

Saturday morning was gloomy, a setting for ghosts and goblins. Fog surrounded the lodge, making trees dim charcoal shapes in the silver mist.

Only Kathleen, Miss Stubblefield, and Mr. Wilkins were in the kitchen when Suzanne got there. The aroma of coffee mixed with that of bacon frying. Miss Stubblefield was placing pieces of bread on a cookie sheet set on the back of an old wood stove.

"Where is everyone?" Suzanne hugged her sweater close, rubbing her arms.

Kathleen was studying a script of *Macbeth* and scribbling in a loose-leaf notebook. "They'll stagger in. Unless you want to walk down the hall and announce breakfast."

"I'd rather have a cup of coffee and get warm. Why aren't the lights on? I practically got dressed in the dark."

"Thank goodness this place has this wood stove." Mr. Wilkins turned bacon in a huge iron skillet. "That storm must have taken out the electricity."

Miss Stubblefield reached for the phone in the

kitchen. "I'll call that Mr. Russell and see if he's working to get the power back. It may go out all the time." She jiggled the buttons over and over. "That's funny. I think the phone is dead."

"Great. I was going to call Jay and give him a list of things I didn't get done before I left." Kathleen sighed. "Well, this is certainly *Macbeth* atmosphere. We'll take advantage of it."

"Hey, there's no electricity," announced Bitsy, entering the kitchen with wet hair. "I couldn't dry my hair."

"I couldn't shave." Right behind her, Willis rubbed a very naked chin.

"Maybe it'll be back on in a couple of years, Willis. Just in time for your beard." Bitsy giggled and grabbed a piece of buttered toast.

"Are you insulting my manhood?" Willis frowned.

"Not that I know of." Bitsy watched Mr. Wilkins lift bacon strips onto a paper towel. "Can I fry myself an egg, Mr. W.?"

"How about I fry up a bunch?" With one hand he cracked eggs quickly into the hot grease.

"Hey, you must be an expert cook." Suzanne was impressed. "I thought only TV cooks could do that."

"Don't ask him how many he splattered onto my kitchen floor before he mastered that trick." Miss Stubblefield picked up the big coffee pot and filled everyone's cup. "This looks like something from my early camping days."

"Did women camp in the eighteen hundreds, Miss S.?" Willis teased.

"Watch your mouth, smart guy, if you want breakfast." Miss Stubblefield might have gray hair,

40

but she was full of spunk. Suzanne had liked her the minute she set eyes on her. Blue eyes sparkled, young and alive and full of mischief.

The rest of the group came in, yawning, still half asleep, complaining about no power. Sol reached for a cup of coffee without speaking. Tamara's damp black curls hung limp around her face, and her eyes were smudged as if her mascara had run.

"You okay, Tam?" asked Suzanne, handing her a cup of black coffee.

She took it gratefully. "I hardly slept, Suzanne. I don't like this place."

"Something kept you awake? What was it?"

"I don't know. I wish we could have been roommates. Why can't we room together, Kathleen?"

"I thought it would be good for each of you to be alone, Tamara. I want you to think about your parts, start to learn lines, get in touch with yourself. Giggling and talking half the night isn't what we're here for."

"I heard someone breaking the rules. Tsk, tsk, tsk." Monica rubbed her two forefingers together. "It was you, Willis, wasn't it? About midnight?"

"If it was, you must have been awake to hear me."

Hank seldom spoke in the morning. He broke his habit to say, "Two eggs, please," then sat by himself, scribbling in a small notebook he carried in his pocket.

"Shhh, genius at work." Willis was going to be his usual irritating self all morning, Suzanne thought. "Roses are dead, violets are too. I'll bring wilted flowers to mourn over you."

"Hey, not bad, Willis." Monica's peal of laugh-

41

ter was almost as wild as that of the loon. "You too can write dark verse."

"Terse verse, hearse verse, worse verse, cursed verse." Now that Willis had started rhyming, he couldn't stop.

Even Kathleen was smiling. One thing you could say for Willis was that it was hard to stay sleepy or gloomy around him.

Suzanne looked at Tamara, and they both collapsed into laughter. "Three cups of coffee and about a dozen of Willis's jokes should start the day with a bang. Hey, where's June?"

"She's always slow." Bitsy shrugged.

"Probably still waiting for her hair dryer to go on." Monica smiled sweetly. "Fortunately I have naturally curly hair." She fluffed her long dark hair and posed.

"I'll go get her," Suzanne volunteered.

"Wait for me." Tamara grabbed the last of her toast and nibbled it as she and Suzanne started down the dim hallway. "I hope it isn't going to rain all weekend. I'm going to lose it cooped up with this bunch."

"I think the rain has stopped. There are low clouds, but isn't that typical around a northern lake?"

"Don't ask me. I'm not the outdoor type."

They entered June's room, but there was no sign of her. Her bed was still a jumble, last night's clothes tossed into a heap on a chair. "June?" Suzanne called.

"I'll check the bathroom." Tamara left and returned almost immediately. "No one in there. You think she went out for a walk this morning?"

"Did she bring several pairs of shoes? There're

her Reeboks from last night. I don't think she'd do that anyway." Suzanne looked in the small closet. June's duffel was on the floor. A couple of shirts were hanging up. "Isn't she always the first one at meals?"

"She does like to eat." Tamara held her hands level with June's bed, running them back and forth.

"What are you doing?"

Tamara looked at Suzanne as if unwilling to tell her. "The bed is pretty cold. I don't think she's been here for a while."

"You can tell?"

"I can—well, sense her presence. Don't ask."

Suzanne couldn't handle that. "Look, Tamara, I'd like to think we're going to be good friends. I like you a lot. You keep suggesting there's something about you that I couldn't understand."

"Or accept."

"Try me. I like to think I'm pretty open."

Tamara stared at Suzanne as if weighing a decision to tell some secrets. Her dark eyes were almost as black as her hair. "I'm pretty psychic. I—well—I know things."

"I understand that. My mom had a friend that read tarot cards at all her parties."

"It's not a game."

"I didn't mean that it was. I think it's a gift."

"Or a curse." Tamara took a deep breath. "But I'm used to it, and I came by it naturally, through my mother and my grandmother. My grandmother and grandfather were Gypsies, Suzanne."

"Really? I thought you were kidding me when you said you had Gypsy blood."

"There aren't many true Gypsies left in this

country. They've mixed with other people. They were persecuted a lot. My grandmother is very powerful, but it brought her a lot of grief."

"So, can you tell where June is? I mean, can you see her, or—what do you know?"

"I just know she hasn't been in this room for some time."

"I came in here with her last night. She was afraid of another of Monica's tricks. That was about ten o'clock. I don't think she'd go wandering around. And it started to storm around midnight."

"I'm picking up on something strange, Suzanne. I have no idea what it is, but I don't like it."

"I'm not the least bit psychic, Tamara, but I've felt funny from the minute we got here and I heard that loon wail. I don't like this place."

"You may be more sensitive than you know. You've just never used it. Everyone has some of those intuitive feelings."

"Let's tell Kathleen. She can decide what to do."

"Sure. Maybe June went outside for some reason and fell. She might be hurt. Maybe we'd better look for her."

Kathleen didn't seem worried or upset when Suzanne reported that June wasn't in her room.

"I heard her crying around one o'clock," said Monica. "I had gotten up to go to the bathroom. I went in her room. She said she'd had a bad dream. I sat there with her for a few minutes. She talked about it, then got quiet. I'm sure she went back to sleep."

Maybe Monica was a better friend to June than

44

Suzanne thought. Despite her spider jokes, June seemed to trust her.

"She'll show up in a little while, I'll bet. But we can go outside and look for her." Sol stood up, then motioned to Hank and Willis.

"Just circle the building while we clean up here," suggested Kathleen. "And call her name."

"If she did go for a walk, she could have gotten lost in this fog. It's as thick as Clyde's cream gravy." Miss Stubblefield watched as Clyde Wilkins stirred the gooey mess in the iron skillet. "Have you never heard of cholesterol, Clyde?"

"My favorite food." Clyde was as slim as the birch trees around the cabins. He didn't seem to worry about what he ate.

When dishes were done, and the searchers returned, Kathleen made a decision. "I can't think where she might have gone off to, but we aren't going to wait all day for her to show up. We can't see the film I brought, but I have a whole list of other things I want us to do."

"Let's get started then," Sol said. "We can give her until noon to put in an appearance. Then we'll really search for her."

"This place is huge. What do you want to bet she moved to another room to sleep and is still counting zees." Willis raised his eyebrows. "And I got up at dawn." He faked a big yawn. "No fair."

Kathleen's first exercise was called a "blind walk." She explained that partners would take turns leading each other around the lodge. One person would be blindfolded and have to trust the other. "Give your partner something to touch, to

45

smell, and even something to taste if you can find anything."

"No way am I putting something in my mouth that Willis gives me," complained Monica. "I'd like a more trustworthy partner."

Kathleen had made them draw slips of paper for partners. "You have to learn to trust everyone here, Monica. You know that. A good cast ensemble is built on trust."

Tamara was partners with Kathleen. Suzanne drew Hank for a partner. She was hoping for Sol, but he went with Bitsy. She found it much easier to lead Hank around than to trust him when it was her turn to be lead.

Without saying a word he tied the bandanna around her eyes, turned her around three times, then took her hand to lead her over a path soft with wet pine needles. She could feel the dampness of the lingering fog on her cheeks, smell the fir and spruce and pine fragrances that perfumed the air.

"Relax, city girl." Hank laughed softly. "I'll take care of you." His touch was gentle, his hand warm on her arm.

She knew they were near the water. She could smell a slight fishy odor, hear the soft lap, lap, lap of tiny waves as they splashed against the shore. She heard a *ker-plunk* of a frog or something diving. Reeds rustled as if something slipped between them.

"Hold out your hand, Lady Macbeth." Hank kept his voice almost to a whisper.

Tentatively, Suzanne turned her hand palm up and toward Hank's voice.

46

"Identify these things."

Coolness, wet. "Water."

Long, stringy, spongy top like a hot dog, but rough. "A cattail!" She laughed and felt pleased that she knew. "You sure don't find those in New York."

She waited and waited. She could hear Hank scrambling about on the shore. "Don't you dare put a frog on my hand, Hank."

He laughed then. "Okay, you win. Besides, I can't catch one." More crunching of his feet on the sand and gravel. Then he took her hand. "Eat this."

"Promise it's okay?"

"Promise."

She opened her mouth. Dry, wrinkled, berrylike. Carefully she nibbled on the object. "It's a blueberry, isn't it?"

"Right. Not many left. This one dried on the bush. I was lucky to find it. I think you pass, lady. It's hard to trust tasting something. Let's go back." He untied the bandanna and it fell from her eyes.

"Oh, where is everything? It's pretty, though, isn't it?"

The fog was even thicker around them. The lake water was black, and no loons floated into view.

"I wonder where the loons are?" Hank said. He had read her mind. "I was hoping one would call in this fog. It would be really eerie, wouldn't it?"

"Uh-huh."

Saying nothing more, they made their way up the hill, following what little path they could see, until they reached the back door of the lodge. Almost everyone was waiting there.

"You left me," Monica screeched. "I trusted you, Willis Hayward, and you left me."

"You finally realized it." Willis thought leaving Monica alone when she was blindfolded was a good joke.

"But I had no idea where I was. I just happened to walk in the right direction. I could have fallen in the lake. I could have walked off a cliff."

"No such luck." Willis ran to escape Monica who took off after him with a wet branch of pine needles.

"All here?" Kathleen said. "Let's go sit in the living room and talk. Ugh. I'm so damp, I'm freezing." She led the way.

"Where's Bitsy?" asked Sol. "She left me alone, too. We should have put Willis and Bitsy together. They deserve each other."

"You were blindfolded?" Hank asked.

"Yes, I called her a few times. Then I took off my bandanna and hiked uphill. It would be pretty hard to get lost unless we'd walked a long way, which we hadn't."

"Something is wrong, Kathleen." Tamara took Kathleen's arm. "June is still gone, and now Bitsy has disappeared."

Kathleen had a funny look on her face. "Maybe Bitsy went to the bathroom. She'll be here in a minute."

"I don't think so." Slowly Tamara shook her head. Then she ducked her head, pressing against her forehead with two fingers. "I have this awful feeling, and—and I'm scared."

Suzanne stepped close and put her arm around Tamara. She could feel her friend trembling, her breath coming in short gasps.

48

"She needs help!" Tamara's voice was full of anguish. "She's asking us to help her." With those words, Tamara slowly crumpled into Suzanne's arms, then slid on down to the floor.

CHAPTER 6

Everyone huddled around them. Suzanne sat on the floor, cradling Tamara's head in her lap.

"Get some water," Kathleen said, kneeling by Suzanne.

"What did she mean, Bitsy needs help?" Lucille Stubblefield clutched a lace-bordered handkerchief to her mouth.

Clyde Wilkins stepped up and put his arm around her. "How could Tamara know where Bitsy is or what she needs?"

"She's—she sees things, feels things." Suzanne didn't know how much to reveal about Tamara.

"You mean she's psychic, really psychic?" Willis asked. "I always thought she was kidding us. I never knew anyone who was really psychic."

"A lot of people are extremely sensitive to the feelings of others." Hank helped Tamara sit up when she started to gain consciousness. "But I thought you had to know that person really well or be kin to them. This fascinates me."

"Look," Suzanne said, "be as fascinated as you want, but if Bitsy does need help, we should start looking for her, don't you think?" Why was every-

50

one being so calm, so matter-of-fact about two missing girls?

"She can't have gone far." Monica pulled a jacket back on. "None of us went far on the walks. Let's break up into teams and search around the lodge."

"Thank you, Monica," Suzanne said. "I'm glad someone is concerned enough to do something besides stand here and talk. As soon as I'm sure Tamara is all right, I'll help you."

Kathleen stood up and took charge. "Let's not forget that we don't know where June is. This puts a different light on her being gone. Maybe whoever—whatever—"

"You think someone like, kidnapped them?" Monica's eyes widened. "I can't believe that."

"Why would anyone want to kidnap June or Bitsy?" Willis asked. "It's not like we're in New York City or Chicago. We're on an island. Criminy, maybe it's some kind of practical joke."

Suzanne looked at each face around her quickly. Could it be? Was this one of Kathleen's exercises?

Tamara sipped the water Hank held for her. "It's not a joke, believe me, it's not. Bitsy was scared."

"Was?" Suzanne clutched Sol's arm.

"When I heard her. I've lost touch." Swinging her feet around, Tamara tried to stand. She had to sit back down.

"Tamara and I will help you look in a few minutes." Suzanne sat beside Tamara. "You guys get started."

"Come on, Willis." Sol motioned. "You and I will go down by the lake."

"Lucille and I will search the lodge," Mr.

Wilkins said. "She doesn't need to be out in this dampness."

"I'm going to go get Mr. Russell." Kathleen started toward the door. "He and his son can help us look for Bitsy and June."

"Maybe two girls shouldn't go out alone." Hank took Monica's arm. "Sol—"

"We're perfectly capable of taking care of ourselves," Suzanne cut him off. She put her hand under Tamara's elbow. "If you're sure you're all right, let's join the searchers."

"A bit wobbly, but it'll pass. Whew, I've been exhausted after I've tapped into someone, but I've never fainted. But, Suzanne, Bitsy's cry for help was so intense. It frightened me."

"Could you get any sense of place or direction?"

"No, it was just there, then gone."

"Was it like she fell or—or was she alone?"

"I don't know that either." Tamara blinked her eyes and took another deep breath. "Let's go outside. Some fresh air sounds good. You know, if whatever happened to her involved someone else—"

"We know all of us. The only people we don't know are Mr. Russell and his son." Suzanne caught the drift of what Tamara was saying.

"And Kathleen said she was going to find Mr. Russell. We shouldn't have let her go off alone."

Outside, Suzanne took Tamara's hand and pulled her along at a half run. She had a vague sense of what direction the caretaker's house was situated in. "His son seems really strange, but it may be because he's been alone so much. I didn't

52

tell you he came and listened to the ghost story last night, did I?"

"I didn't see him."

"I don't think anyone did, except me. He got close enough to hear, then hid. I was wishing we could invite him into the fire circle, but I was afraid he'd run if we spoke to him."

There was a well-worn path through the woods, so they stayed on it until a small house, almost a cottage, jumped up out of the mist.

"Maybe this is a better idea than we thought." Suzanne stopped to tell Tamara her idea. "If you could meet this boy again, you might be able to sense something. You might know if he's connected to June's and Bitsy's disappearance."

"I might. We never should have ignored the fact that June was gone this morning."

"You're right, Tamara. But I don't know her well. For all I knew, you guys had some inside information. Like, she goes off alone a lot of the time. Some people are moody and have habits like that. Even though June doesn't seem like that type of person. Hank does, but not June."

They met Kathleen, Mr. Russell, and his son coming out of the cabin. Kathleen was surprised to see them. "Did you find Bitsy?" She was prepared to be relieved. "And how about June?"

How to put this so as not to insult Mr. Russell? Suzanne didn't much care. "No. We came after you because we decided you shouldn't have gone off alone. Are they going to help us?"

"Yes. They know the island better than we do. "Andy, this is Tamara and Suzanne. They're in the play we're working on." Kathleen introduced Mr. Russell's son.

Andy didn't speak, but he didn't seem afraid like he had in the lodge. He nodded his head and glanced quickly at the two girls. Then he motioned to his father that he was leaving.

"Sure, Andy, search the other cabins." Mr. Russell tossed a big ring of keys toward Andy. "Look inside each of them."

"Should he go off alone?" Suzanne asked.

"He lives out here year-round," Mr. Russell reminded them. "He knows every inch of the island."

"Is he autistic?" asked Kathleen.

"I don't know what that is." Mr. Russell snapped a huge flashlight off and on.

"You never had him tested to see why he didn't speak?" Suzanne was amazed.

"His mother and I were quiet people. She died when Andy was three. I got this job out here right away. We're happy here."

"He's never been in school?"

Kathleen looked at Suzanne and her face said, leave this alone for now. It's not our business.

"You girls go down that way." Mr. Russell pointed. "There's horse stables and riding paths. "Me and Ms. Reed will go into the woods a little ways. If this girl got lost in this pea soup, surely she'll stay put until she hears us yelling."

The minute they were alone, Suzanne felt cold. She pulled her light jacket close over her sweater and buttoned it all the way up. It was the dampness. The temperature probably wasn't that low.

Tamara took Suzanne's arm after a couple of minutes. "I don't know about you, but I don't want to get separated out here. I don't have a very good sense of direction."

54

"Don't you look on the side of a tree for moss, and that's north?" Suzanne had no woods experience at all. She was never a Girl Scout and her family wasn't outdoorsy.

"Yeah, I heard that, too. But which side? And look at this tree. There's moss all over it."

They heard the horses before they saw the stables. There were sounds of blowing and soft nickering and the jingle of harness. Suzanne breathed in the rich odor of hay and manure and damp animals.

The noises picked up when the stable door creaked. There was stamping and pawing and bumping of stable walls.

"They think we're going to feed them."

"Sorry, girls," Suzanne said, peering into each of the stalls. They were warm and cozy with hay beds and old blankets thrown around.

"How do you know they're all girls?" Tamara asked from across the row.

"They're mares or neutral, if kids ride them a lot. I think. I'm no expert, but there are stables in Central Park. I didn't like the lessons, but I have been on a horse before."

"I haven't. June? Bitsy?" Tamara called. "We should be calling them. If they can hear us."

"What do you mean by that?" Suzanne jumped right onto Tamara's remark.

"Nothing. Let's just call out."

"You didn't feel anything else? They aren't—"

"I don't know. I'm not feeling anything but cold. Let's holler outside, then go back and see if anyone had any luck. Maybe they're in the lodge by now."

"You'll tell me everything you know, won't you, Tamara?"

"Hey, get off my case. Of course I will. But I'm not magic."

They walked a few minutes in silence. There weren't any sounds except their soft footsteps.

"I'm sorry. I know you aren't. I'm scared, Tamara. Really scared."

"Okay, here's the truth. So am I."

Grasping hands, they ran all the way to the lodge, up the steps, and into the big living room. A welcome blast of warm air hit them. Someone had the fire roaring.

Suzanne's relief at being back didn't last long, however. Everyone was huddled around Willis, who was holding a wet towel to his head. Everyone that is, except Kathleen and Mr. Russell and—

"Where's Sol?" Suzanne asked.

"He's gone!" Willis was no longer the funny man. In fact, he was on the verge of tears. "Someone hit me over the head. When I came to, Sol had disappeared."

CHAPTER 7

S ol gone? Suzanne felt as if she'd been hit in the stomach. She turned away and jammed her fist to her mouth to keep her breakfast down. After several deep breaths, she yelled at Willis before she could stop herself. "Why didn't you keep your eye on him? How could you let this happen?"

"He didn't let it happen, Suzanne." Hank placed his hand on Suzanne's arm and squeezed. "It's not his fault."

"Why did someone hit me and take Sol?" Willis asked. "Why not hit Sol and take me?" Willis seemed close to hysteria, as if he, too, blamed himself.

Tamara placed her hand on Willis's shoulder. "He only wanted Sol. This time."

"This time?" Suzanne stared at Tamara. She looked pale and shaken. "You think there's going to be another? That someone is planning this?"

"Remember that play we did two years ago, Kathleen?" Willis still held the wet towel to his head. *Ten Little Indians.* People kept disappearing one by one."

"Until there were none," Monica added. "One, then none."

"We sure aren't going to stand around and let that happen." Clyde Wilkins stood up and started to pace the floor.

"That's for sure. No one is to go anyplace alone." Kathleen started giving orders. "And—"

Willis reminded her. "Sol and I didn't go out alone."

"We'll lock up the lodge and stay inside then. All of us."

"Why don't we just call the police?" Monica asked. "That's the logical thing to do."

"The phones are all out," Lucille reminded them. "Last night's storm that knocked out the electricity knocked out the phones, too."

"Don't you have a boat, Mr. Russell? For going to the mainland for supplies?" Hank came alive. "We can't all go at once like we came in, but we'll just leave here and call the police from the mainland."

Russell shook his head. "I sent the boy to check on the boat early this morning, after the storm. It was still tied up, but there was a huge hole in the bottom. Someone made sure we can't leave."

"Then—then this *is* planned." Suzanne stared at Tamara.

"How about a two-way radio?" Hank asked. "Surely you have one. The power must go out a lot in the winter."

"That, too. Someone smashed it."

Suzanne stared at the caretaker. Someone. Was it Russell? Or his son? Should they take his word for the damage? Demand to see the radio or the boat? Who was doing this? She spoke her thoughts. "Let's think about who might be trying to frighten us."

58

"Or worse," Miss Stubblefield added.

Kathleen wanted her group alone. "Mr. Russell, you know the island. Will you and your son keep looking? Then you can come back here if you want to. We have plenty of food. Show yourself, and we'll unlock the doors."

They all watched Russell leave, and Hank locked the front door behind him.

"You forget he has keys to every place here," said Suzanne. Locking the door didn't make her feel safe. "He can get into the lodge anytime he wants, day or night."

"I wanted us to be able to talk without him," said Kathleen. She sat beside Willis on the couch.

"Then you suspect him?" Hank asked.

"I think it's his weird son doing this." Monica huddled in a overstuffed rocker. "Maybe he's gone bananas being out here alone for so long."

"That's just it," Kathleen pointed out. "The caretaker and his son have been here a long time. When I booked the reservation, Mrs. Gordon said they were very reliable and would help us in any way we needed."

"Someone can be reliable one day and lose it the next." Willis folded the damp towel carefully. There was a nasty bruise, turning dark, on the side of his forehead.

"Andy seemed eager to help, to search when his father sent him off," Suzanne said. "There's something about him that won't let me believe he's crazy enough to—to kidnap people."

"We're not the only actors in the world," Hank said scribbling in his notebook.

What could he be writing down? Suzanne thought. She had gotten used to his carrying what was probably a journal all the time. Was he taking notes on their predicament? It made her uncomfortable to think she was a character in the story he was recording.

"Okay, we know none of us is doing this, even for a joke." Kathleen approached the situation logically, as if it were an acting problem they were facing. "Who else is left except Mr. Russell and his son?"

"Easy." Monica shrugged. "Someone could have hidden over here all week, just waiting for us to show up."

"You don't mean *us,* just whatever group showed up next. Right?" Hank added to Monica's thinking.

"Remember that mass murderer who was also a cannibal?" Willis blurted out.

"Willis!" Miss Stubblefield scolded him like he was a two-year-old. "Mercy me. Isn't this bad enough without you letting your imagination run wild?"

Willis looked sheepish and grinned. "Sorry. It just slipped out."

Everyone laughed a little, but no one could think Willis's remark funny. Suzanne was glad he was over his panic enough to joke, though.

"Tamara." Suzanne hated to do this to Tam, but they had to do something. She couldn't stand sitting and waiting. "Can you see things when you try—like go into a trance or something and ask questions?"

"Let's have a séance." Monica's laughter started deep and bubbled up like the loon's rich yodel.

Both Tamara and Suzanne gave her a disgusted look.

"Well, you suggested it. I think it's a great idea." Monica tossed her long dark hair over her shoulder and started pulling chairs around a table.

"I've never tried that," Tamara said. "And I don't know that I want to." She stayed seated firmly on the couch beside Willis.

He took her arm. "What can it hurt, Tam? You never know. You might get some vibes. You might be even more powerful than you think."

"I know all about my powers, Willis. I've lived with them for a long time."

Everyone stood waiting to hear Tamara explain her ability, but she hadn't meant she was going to do so.

"This is really private, and I'm not willing to put on a show for you people." Something was making Tamara angry.

"I don't think I can handle this anyway." Miss Stubblefield struggled up from her chair. "I'm going to lie down for a little while."

"I'll go with you to your room." Mr. Wilkins started to follow her.

"You'll do no such thing. I'm perfectly capable of getting to my room from here. You fix lunch, Clyde. I've never known anything to make young people lose their appetites." Miss Stubblefield headed for the hallway.

Kathleen grinned. "They act like an old married couple, don't they?"

Her remark helped them relax a little. Tamara ran her fingers through tangled curls. "Okay, I'll try, but I don't promise anything."

Suzanne felt silly sitting in the circle around the table. She guessed that everyone did. "Do we hold hands?"

"It will make us stronger if we bond that way," Kathleen suggested.

For what seemed like a long time, they sat quietly, the only sound the crackling of the fire. Suzanne kept trying to clear her mind, to think of nothing. All she could think about, though, was the look of terror on June's face when her bed was full of spiders. Where was she? Was she locked up someplace, some old shed or something, someplace where there might be insects. Was she terrified right now? Or was she even conscious, aware of anything? Suzanne didn't want to use the word *dead*, but it came to her. And Sol, sweet, sensitive Sol. She wanted him here, beside her, his arm around her again. She wanted the chance to tell him she liked him—a lot.

"I can't do this anymore!" Her breath and the statement came out in a rush, almost a scream as she jumped to her feet.

"That's okay, Suzanne. I'm not getting any messages, any *vibes*, Willis, nothing." Tamara stood up, both hands flat on the table. "I'm sorry. I more often see things when I'm not trying to. They come unbidden. I guess I could work more on making them come, but I—I haven't."

Suzanne calmed down and put her arm around Tamara. "You haven't wanted to, have you, Tamara?"

"No. I didn't want to be this way, Suzanne." Tamara started to cry softly. "My mother tried to help me accept it as normal. My grandmother said it was a gift. She wanted to teach me, but I refused. I didn't want it!"

Suzanne waved everyone away. "You could help

people with it, Tamara. It is a gift, a talent. Just like music or art or acting, or—"

"Are you telling me to grow up, Suzanne?" Tamara wiped her eyes and blew her nose on a tissue. "That's what my mother finally said to me."

"No, I think you have to accept it in your own time. When you want to. Let's move your things into my room. I don't care what Kathleen says, we're bunking together. I'm not staying alone one more minute."

"That's the best idea anyone has had today."

Kathleen had sent people to wash up for lunch or help in the kitchen, so no one was in the hall when Tamara and Suzanne got Tamara's small suitcase, her tape recorder, and a basket purse of personal items.

Suzanne stood at the window while Tamara got settled in the opposite bottom bunk. "The fog is lifting. It would have been a beautiful day."

"What do you think is happening here, Suzanne?" Tamara came to stand beside her. The lake came into view. Sunlight filtered down through the disappearing clouds like a celestial backdrop.

"I can't even imagine."

"Let's promise not to lose sight of each other at any time. We'll even go to the bathroom together."

"And no showers." Suzanne tried to laugh. They both knew what movie she made reference to, and Suzanne had seen all the copycat scenes since. But those movies weren't real. This was real. She wasn't going to be able to go home and forget about it. Actors that had gotten killed weren't going to come back and take a bow when the play was over.

A loon's cry echoed across the lake, reminding

Suzanne of Hank's earlier words. "Hank said the Indians believed the loon's cry announces dying, precedes the death."

"That sounds like something Hank would say or know about. Let's get back to the kitchen. I don't feel like eating, but I'd rather be in a crowd right now."

Suzanne agreed, and they hurried back down the hall.

Kathleen seemed relieved to see the pair when they entered the kitchen. "I can't help but do a head count every five minutes," she admitted. "I can't handle anyone else disappearing."

"Where are the over-the-hill lovers?" Willis had recovered enough to joke about the two people absent from their group.

"Clyde went to call Lucille to lunch."

Everyone loaded their plates and started to eat. Willis was keeping track of time, it seemed. "Haven't they been gone a long time? Not that they don't deserve some privacy for donating their weekend to chaperon, but if we're going to keep track of everyone they have to follow the rules, don't they?"

Kathleen smiled. "Let's you and I go get them, Will. I'll peek in first just in case."

There were a lot of uncensored remarks about nooners and senior citizen love affairs after Kathleen and Willis left. Not that she couldn't handle straight talk from the play cast or their off-color remarks, but some of the joking was done to relieve the tension that was starting to build.

Suzanne's stomach cramped around the undigested sandwich she'd eaten before Kathleen and

64

Willis reappeared. One look at her face told the story.

"They're gone."

"Both of them," Willis added, biting his lower lip. "And there's blood on Miss Stubblefield's pillow."

CHAPTER 8

Tamara started to cry softly. "I'm sorry, I'm sorry," she kept saying over and over. Suzanne didn't know why she didn't feel like crying or screaming, but for some reason—shock maybe—she found herself studying the reaction of everyone in the room.

She remembered a small poster she kept on the bulletin board in her room. *If you can keep your cool when everyone around you is going to pieces, maybe you don't understand the situation.*

She certainly didn't understand why this was happening, but the situation was simple. One by one, and now two by two, people in her group were disappearing. She stared at Kathleen. Could this be one of her theater games? she wondered again. Was she having people hide in order to see the reaction of the rest of the cast? It seemed like a crazy thing to do, but Tamara and others had told her Kathleen did some wild and crazy things on these weekends. Some of her bonding exercises were creative and imaginative. If she wanted those who were being left to bond to each other, she had hit on to the best game ever.

Hank circled Suzanne's shoulders with his arm

66

and pulled her close to him. "Are you all right, Suzanne? You have a strange look on your face."

"I—I think it must be disbelief." She lowered her voice. "Hank, do you think this is one of Kathleen's games? Did she plan this to see how we'd react?"

"Now that's an angle I hadn't thought of. Good thinking." A smile came over his face. "She's never pulled anything this crazy before, but it's not impossible. If that's the case, though, I think it's gone far enough."

"Yes, I agree. How can we find out?"

"Simple. Ask her." He stood up. "Okay, Kathleen Reed, me beauty. The game is over. We've enjoyed it. It was great while it lasted, but we've found you out."

"What are you talking about, Hank?" Kathleen stared at him.

Monica broke into peals of laughter. "Oh, Kathleen, I love it. You didn't! Why haven't I thought of that?" She jumped up, tossed her head back, and laughed her maniacal laugh, screeching and weaving like a willow in the wind. " 'Fair is foul, and foul is fair. Hover through the fog and filthy air.' The fog is clearing." She pointed a long finger with its scarlet nail at Kathleen. "The fog is lifting; the air is coming clear. We have found you out, dear teacher. Foul, foul deed." Again she laughed, sending shivers up Suzanne's back.

The role of witch suited Monica perfectly. And for the first time, Suzanne wondered why Kathleen had given her the part of Lady Macbeth over this talented actress.

"Whew, are we having any fun yet? Good show, Monica and Kathleen." Willis visibly relaxed and collapsed into his place at the table. "More Coke, please, someone." He held up an empty glass. "Thank goodness you figured this out, Hank."

Putting her hands on her hips, Kathleen protested. "Hey, people, wait a minute. You think this is some kind of game I've thought up for the weekend's entertainment?"

Suzanne hadn't seen Kathleen get angry yet. She'd heard about the teacher's temper, but hadn't witnessed it. "You didn't stage this, Kathleen?" she asked quietly. *Oh, please say this is a game.*

"No lying, Kathleen." Willis held up both hands. "It's all right; we'll forgive you."

"I know nothing about what's happening out here. Do you really think I'd try to scare you this way?"

"Yes," Hank answered honestly. "We've learned to expect anything when we go off with you."

"Well, I give you credit for being open to my experiments, but this isn't one of them." Kathleen shuddered and sat down. "This is real. I'd like to hear any of your ideas."

It took a few minutes for the group to believe Kathleen. It had been such an easy answer to what was fast becoming a nightmare.

"There's some crazy stranger out here with us?" It was both statement and question. Suzanne had said it for all of them.

"What if it's not a stranger?" Hank posed another question.

Tamara twisted a ring 'round and 'round on her finger. "You mean, it's one of us?"

Monica grinned. "That's almost as good an idea as Kathleen doing it. Someone is paying you back, Kathleen, for all those times you've made us do

68

crazy things. All those times you got us to bare our souls. How do you like it?"

"Hey, Monica, get off her case," Hank said. "She said this isn't her idea. I believe her. I just threw out the possibility."

"What if—what if—" Tamara stuttered. "What if there's a killer here on the island with us?"

No one had an answer for that question. They all got very quiet considering it. Suzanne shivered and hugged herself tightly.

Hank had a list in his notebook. Suzanne could see that much, but his handwriting was so bad, she couldn't make out what it said. Was it a list of the people who had disappeared? Was it a list of the whole cast, and he was ticking them off as they left? Hank with his obsession with death—could he have lost it, decided to do some crazy experiment to see how each one of them would react? He was writing this all up in his journal. Maybe he planned to write a paper for psychology class about what was happening.

Suzanne! she scolded herself. Get control of your imagination. The mad scientist went out with Dr. Frankenstein. But it was certainly possible that one of them was causing the others to disappear. She studied each person left at the table in turn.

Willis? It would be hard to believe, but he said he had all that junk inside him. He loved telling jokes, but he wasn't as much of a practical joker as Monica was. And June seemed to have been the butt of all of Monica's jokes. Could Willis have run out of jokes as a way of expressing his anger and loneliness? Could his hatred for his parents have spread out to include everyone around him? The idea seemed really far-fetched but possible.

Monica? She was jealous and spoiled and she wanted her own way all the time, but a killer? Suzanne would have to really stretch her imagination to believe that. Monica loved to pick on people—underdogs—she was really a bully. Bullies were usually guys, but not always. But bullies were usually cowards at heart, too. Unhappy people who take out their anger on others.

Kathleen had already denied that this was a joke, and the stricken look on her face when she'd returned to say Miss Stubblefield and Mr. Wilkins were gone would garner her an Oscar nomination if she were acting. Suzanne didn't think she'd go this far with her theater games.

Tamara? Suzanne smiled at the idea. She'd as soon believe she, herself, would do something like this. Tamara's saying she was sorry over and over suggested guilt, but it was guilt that she was no help in discovering the real culprit here. Guilt that she knew she had this power but couldn't use it to help them.

That left the caretaker, Mr. Russell, and his son, Andy. What motive could they have for scaring the play cast or hurting all the people who were gone? Could Andy's antisocial behavior have grown worse without his father knowing it? Could the boy have developed some sort of psychotic personality because of his isolation on the island? Maybe after the summer groups had left, he'd decided he didn't want anyone else disturbing them.

"Maybe it's the curse of doing *Macbeth*," Suzanne said aloud, without realizing it until everyone looked at her.

"We need to stay busy." Kathleen ignored the remark and took charge of the group again. She

70

stood, walked over to the corner of the room, and came back with a big box. "Hank, will you and Willis get those other two boxes? We're going to all stay right here in the kitchen, and to keep our minds and hands busy, we're going to make masks to wear in the play. The boat will come for us tomorrow. And maybe when my husband calls and calls and realizes the power is out, he'll come or call and send someone early to find out if we're okay. Someone must have tried to call us. They'll know there was a storm and that the lines are down."

"Maybe someone will have tried the radio, too. That woman who rents this place would know how to contact us in an emergency." Willis came back wearing a black cloak with a hood from the costume box. He set down his box and started to dig in it. "Hey, neat stuff." He took out a black ostrich feather and stuck it in his hair. "On guard, d'Artagnan. Prepare to defend your honor." He pulled a small dagger from the box and started an imaginary sword fight all around the kitchen.

Suzanne laughed in spite of herself. And she was glad for Willis's ability to play the fool. Wasn't the traditional role of the comic to take people's minds off their troubles? If they ever needed a fool it was now.

"I'm going to make the mask for the ghost," said Kathleen, setting the tone for working. "Let's stir up a batch of papier-mâché. Suzanne, see if you can find a big pot. Here's some wallpaper paste." She handed Suzanne a sack.

Putting her mind only on her immediate task, Suzanne rummaged in the cupboards, making lots of noise—somehow that made her feel better—

and then mixed up the sweet-smelling batch of goo. She brought it back to the kitchen table, which had now become a worktable, tore strips of newspaper, and started shaping a mask for herself.

After a couple of hours, during which people talked about the play, their roles, or social life at school carefully avoiding the present, Monica spoke up. "Are we all going to go to the bathroom together?" She had a naughty grin on her face.

"Suits me." Willis held up a goopy, distorted face in front of his own. "I won't peek if you girls won't."

"All of the women will go together first," Kathleen decided, "then you two men."

"I liked Monica's idea better." Willis pouted. "Maybe I don't want to be alone with Hank."

Maybe Willis wasn't entirely kidding. But that's what they did, and everyone came back safely.

"Let's all drag our mattresses into the living room tonight." Kathleen leaned her mask on the back of the big wood stove to dry. "There are candles in the drawer over there, and I assume you all have flashlights. I'm determined that not one more of us is going to disappear."

"Half can sleep at once, and we'll take turns keeping the fire going and watching." Hank finished Kathleen's plan.

The plan seemed good, and Suzanne felt safer because of it. It should work. She was in total agreement with Kathleen. She couldn't handle one more person disappearing.

They fixed dinner, and even though everyone said he or she couldn't eat, the food disappeared. They all helped clean the kitchen, the dishes, and the mess from the mask-making project.

When they were all settled into the living room, fully dressed, but with beds scattered around the room, Suzanne relaxed even more. She could feel that everyone else had done so too. The routine of eating, getting ready to sleep, and of keeping to some of the projects they'd planned for the weekend helped them push aside the worry they all had for their four missing friends.

"Ooops, did I floss?" Willis said, squinting one eye, trying to remember.

"Tough, Hayward," Hank answered him. "I'm not going back to the bathroom with you. You'll just have to be a social outcast by morning." He blew out the candle he'd set beside his sleeping bag.

"Do you think we could set traps across each doorway with dental floss?" Willis couldn't or wouldn't settle down.

"Will you shut up?" Monica raised onto one elbow. "You're on first watch. Try it if that will keep you quiet."

Two minutes later Willis spoke again. "Are we having any fun yet?" There was a plaintive tone to his voice. "Shut up, Willis!" Tamara wasn't teasing. Willis got quiet.

Suzanne lay and watched the shadows wandering about the room. Some were from the fire's crackling blaze, some from candles left burning on end tables and the mantel. The old building creaked as it settled for the night. A slight breeze had come up, and occasionally a down draft would cause the flames to sputter and spit.

She could swear there were footsteps outside the front windows, as if someone was creeping across the long wraparound porch. Suddenly there was a rapping at the front door, then the click of a key in the lock, and the door slammed open.

"Who is it?" Kathleen was on her feet immediately. Hank and Willis dashed to stand beside her.

"Charlie Russell. Sorry if I woke you. I could see all the lights, though. I figured you were still up."

"We're all going to sleep here, then stay together until the boat comes tomorrow. What do you want?" There was a note of distrust in Kathleen's voice. Had she decided the caretaker was to blame for their mystery? If so, she changed her mind with Mr. Russell's next words.

"I was looking for my boy. Andy. Have you seen him? Has he been up here?"

Tamara took hold of Suzanne's arm, and the two moved closer. They had already made their beds side by side. "How long since you saw him, Mr. Russell?" Tamara asked.

"I—I don't know. I'm so used to his going and coming as he pleases. Sometimes he stays gone for hours. There ain't no trouble he can get into here, and he likes watching the animals. I was tinkering with the radio, trying to fix it back together." Mr. Russell was visibly shaken by Andy's absence. "But he comes home at night. He always sleeps in his room."

"Did you see him after he went looking into the other cabins this morning?" Suzanne tried to think logically.

The man turned an old felt hat round and round by the brim. "I guess I haven't, now that you mention it. I lose track of time sometimes myself."

"And we're losing track of people," Tamara

74

muttered, just loud enough for Suzanne to hear. Had she said it to herself or to all of them?

It didn't matter. They were all very aware of that fact. They'd come out here with eleven people. Two lived here. That made thirteen, the classic unlucky number. And only seven were left.

CHAPTER 9

How could six people just disappear into the fog on an island? It was a question that Suzanne kept asking herself over and over, but she knew she really didn't want an answer. She just wanted whatever was happening to stop.

"I'm sorry, Mr. Russell," Kathleen said. "We haven't seen him since this morning either. Would you like to stay here with us tonight? We'll find a space for you."

"No, ma'am. I aim to keep looking until I find him." Placing his felt hat back onto his head, Mr. Russell left through the front door again.

Before Kathleen could lock the door behind him, Hank was there, holding his boots and socks, one arm into his jacket. "I'm going to help him look, Kathleen. It's better than lying here waiting for something to happen."

"Maybe you shouldn't, Hank." Kathleen's voice was hesitant. "I am responsible for all of you."

Hank smiled. "Have you been able to protect us so far?"

Kathleen looked stricken. She started to shake her head. "No, no, I haven't. I'm sorry, I'm so

76

sorry." She bit her bottom lip and leaned on the door.

"Want to come along, Willis?" Hank invited. "There's supposed to be safety in numbers." He laughed.

Willis looked surprised that Hank even invited him. "I—I guess I'll stay here. Monica and I have first watch. And maybe I'll be safe with all these women." It seemed to be getting harder and harder for Willis to joke, but he was trying.

"Right. It's a tough job, but someone has to guard them." Laughing again, Hank slipped out the door. "Russell, wait up," he called. "I'm coming with you."

Kathleen locked the door securely, shooting the top bolt this time, then testing both. For a moment, she leaned against it again. Then she walked slowly back across the room, standing by the fire, staring into it, as if there were some answers in the flames. No one could think of anything to say. Finally she returned to her mattress. "All we have to do is get through this night. Tomorrow we'll go sit on the beach until the boat comes."

"No way can I sleep," Tamara said, sitting on her bed.

"Me either." Suzanne lay down anyway. She was tired, exhausted by the day's events, but fear was keeping her mind alert. Slowly, though, very slowly, she relaxed, and then, without meaning to, she slept deeply.

It took Tamara a long time to shake her awake. "Suzanne, Suzanne, wake up. Please, wake up."

"What? Oh, leave me alone. I'm so tired. Just let me sleep a few minutes longer. Then I'll make my mask. I know just what color I want it."

77

"Suzanne, you're dreaming. Wake up!" Tamara was pounding on her back now, since Suzanne had rolled over, pulling her blanket tightly around her.

"Oh, oh, what's wrong, Tamara? I didn't mean to go to sleep, but I couldn't help it. It's morning. We made it, Tamara, we made it through the night. Get up, everyone, we made it. Let's pack up and go down the to beach and wait like Kathleen said."

Kathleen sat up slowly on hearing her name. "Why didn't anyone wake me? I was supposed to have the second watch. Willis, why didn't you wake me. Willis?"

"He's gone, Ms. Reed." Tamara's voice was formal, monotone, like a bad telephone recording. "And so is Monica."

"Both of them?" Suzanne hoped she was still dreaming. Her night had been full of masks, people wearing masks—all colors, shapes, sizes. She couldn't identify any of them. They kept floating around her, in and out of the fog, calling her name. She shook her head, wishing she hadn't remembered.

"The three of us are alone, since who knows where Hank is," Tamara started for the kitchen.

"Wait!" Suzanne stopped her. "Where are you going?"

"I'm going to the bathroom. Then I'm going to make a cup of tea. I'm not afraid anymore. It's silly to be afraid. Someone is preying on our fear. It feeds them, it feeds them." Tamara continued from the room chanting the last phrase.

"Has she lost her mind?" Suzanne scrambled to her feet. "Kathleen, come on. We have to go with her."

Kathleen followed Suzanne, but she seemed to

78

be in as much of a daze as Tamara. "A cup of tea sounds great."

Back in the kitchen, they moved like robots, starting a fire in the old cook stove—there was still no power. Tamara filled a pan from bottled water she'd brought to drink, not trusting the camp's water, she had told Suzanne on the boat trip over.

A million years ago. Suzanne tried to bring back their mood, the laughing and teasing, the anticipation of fun and hard work to get a production started.

"I guess we won't get to do the play." What a stupid thing for her to say, to worry about right now. It just slipped out.

"I never should have chosen *Macbeth*. It has been a long time since we did *Romeo and Juliet*. We could have done that easily. I have all my notes from the last production."

"Bitsy would have made a good Juliet. She's so tiny and pretty." Suzanne imagined her in the role. Playing opposite Sol, of course. He'd have gotten any of the male leads.

They kept a conversation going about Shakespeare's plays, as if this were any morning, as if none of the weekend had happened. Suzanne finally realized, though, that she and Kathleen were doing all the talking. Tamara was intent on making tea, as if she could concentrate on only one thing at a time.

She found a large tray, got out a big teapot with yellow roses on it. There were no cups to match, but the mugs they had washed last night were on the drain board. "Three cups, three spoons, three napkins, three tea bags, for three guests. Let's go back into the living room by the fire."

Suzanne started to worry about Tamara. She wasn't herself at all. They followed her, carrying the tray, and watched her set it on a low table. Kathleen hurried to stir up some embers and place kindling on them. She blew until a small thread of flame leaped into the stack and set it burning with pops and cracks.

They all stared at the fire while they sipped the amber liquid and nibbled Granola bars that Tamara had broken into small bite-sized pieces. Making the breakfast last as long as possible, they kept pretending that nothing bad had happened, that the three of them had come here alone. Or at least, it seemed that way. Suzanne knew she didn't want to think about what to do next. What could they do?

"Did you see the sign?" said Tamara, finally.

"What sign?" Kathleen became alert.

"By Willis's bed." Tamara went to get it. She held it up for Suzanne and Kathleen to read.

In bold black letters, painted with blood red tempera from their box of supplies were the words, ARE WE HAVING ANY FUN YET?

"How awful." Kathleen buried her head in both hands.

"It does tell us one thing," Suzanne pointed out.

"What's that?" Tamara lay the sign on the tea tray.

"Someone knew he said that all the time."

"Someone has been watching us ever since we got here? Anyone could have overheard him saying it. I think he said it every five minutes." Tamara snapped out of her trancelike state with the

80

statement. "I don't know about you two, but I'm getting angry."

"At who?" Suzanne would be happy to get angry, but who should she direct it toward?

"At myself. I'm ready to try to find out what's happening here."

"What do you mean? What are you going to do?" Kathleen was as confused as Suzanne.

"Maybe the séance—if you want to call it that—didn't work because there were too many people around me. I'm going to try again."

"What can you find out? I don't really understand what you're going to do."

"Suzanne, I know you think this is weird, and I think it is, too, but I'm just going to concentrate, to try to see or hear something, get some information."

"Dial oh for operator—ask for information?" It was a lame joke. Suzanne missed Willis.

"I'm willing to try anything." Kathleen joined them.

The folded their legs and sat in a circle on the rug in front of the fireplace. Tamara held out both her hands and connected with Suzanne and Kathleen.

"Just sit quietly. I—I'll do my best." Tamara relaxed, shut her eyes, and let her chin fall forward.

The fire burned low, but still popped occasionally. There was no other sound, not even of their breathing. Suzanne watched Tamara, the slow rise and fall of her chest, her long, dark lashes resting on pale, ivory skin. Her hair, looking as if it hadn't been combed for days, tumbled about her face and onto her shoulders.

"I'm asking for information," Tamara whispered

after a few minutes of silence. "I've never asked before, but you've given it to me anyway. This time I'm asking. Please, let me know something."

Suzanne wished she could ask Tamara who she thought she was talking to. Was it God, or whatever you wanted to call the Power in the universe? Maybe Tamara didn't even know. Maybe she didn't care. She just knew she got information someplace, at unexpected times.

Tears rolled down Tamara's cheeks. Before she could stop herself, Suzanne squeezed her hand. "What?" she whispered. "What, Tamara?"

"Fear. I feel a great deal of fear. Almost everyone is afraid. I—I think one person is not."

"That makes sense. It's the person responsible. Tamara, if people are afraid, they're still alive." Kathleen looked relieved.

"They're watching—watching—"

"Who's watching?" Suzanne looked around the room and toward the front windows. "Someone is watching us?"

"I don't know. I see that word. I hear that word. Just *watching.*" Tamara wilted and started to shiver violently.

Kathleen jumped up and ran to get a blanket. She brought it back and wrapped it around Tamara's shoulders, holding her close.

"Don't try anymore, Tamara," she said. "This scares me, too, for you to do this. I know it happens. I don't disbelieve that you can feel things, maybe see things we can't see. But it scares me just the same."

Tamara started to cry harder. She knotted the blanket in her fists and tugged it tighter. "They're so afraid, Suzanne. They're all so scared."

"We'll find them." Suzanne scooted around and held Tamara in her arms. "Now that we know they're alive, we'll find them. We'll help them." It was an empty promise, but Suzanne didn't know what else to say.

There was a pounding at the front door. Hank leaned around and peered into the window, then rapped on it with his fingers.

Suzanne ran to let him in. He looked awful—muddy, red eyed, exhausted. "Oh, Hank, some good news. They're alive. Right now they're all still alive. Let's look. Get a cup of coffee and help us look some more. We've got to find them!"

CHAPTER 10

Finding out that their friends were still alive gave them new hope of being able to find them.

"I just can't understand why someone would want to do this—take people off and lock them up someplace." Kathleen tried to puzzle out what had happened while she made coffee for Hank.

"Is that what's happening?" Hank asked. "You have it all figured out?"

"Well, that's how it looks."

Hank also didn't believe the way they'd received their information. "How could Tamara know what is happening?"

"She felt it, sensed it," Suzanne tried to explain again. "Someone tells her things."

"Who. God? Someone sitting up there in the sky watching everything we're doing down here. Laughing at how inadequate human beings are?"

Kathleen didn't want to continue this discussion. "Hank, you're tired. Drink some coffee and eat something. We'll get ready to go back out with you."

"We covered a lot of the island, but I can't say as it did a lot of good, tramping around out there in the dark. Mr. Russell seemed to always know where he was going."

"Hey, my mask is gone." Kathleen pointed. "I left it on the back of the stove to dry."

"What difference does it make, Kathleen?" Tamara seemed almost as tired as Hank. "You weren't going to finish it, were you?"

"I don't know," Kathleen admitted. "Right now, I don't know anything. I can't plan very far ahead."

Suzanne, Tamara, and Kathleen got shoes and jackets on and waited for Hank to say he was ready. Suzanne was eager to be active. Just sitting and waiting for something to happen, or not happen, was getting to her.

The sky was overcast, another storm approaching. It was cool and damp. At first, Suzanne wished she had two sweaters on, but walking helped her get warm.

"Let's see if Mr. Russell wants to go with us," suggested Hank. "He knows the island better than we do."

They headed in the direction of the caretaker's cabin. Walking single file down the narrow pathway, no one spoke. The door to the cabin stood open. Hank knocked, then stepped inside. "Mr. Russell? We're going back out to search again. Are you still here?"

No sound came from the interior. Hank walked all the way in and was gone a couple of minutes.

"He's not here. I guess he checked to see if Andy had come back, then took off again to continue looking."

"Are you sure?" Tamara asked. "Maybe—"

"*I'm* not a mind reader." Hank slammed the front door. "I'm guessing that's what happened."

"Hank, is there something you're not telling us?" Kathleen put her hand on his arm. "Why are you so angry at us? We're all in this mess together."

Hank squeezed his fingers into fists and swung at the air in front of him. "I just feel so helpless. If this is someone's idea of a joke, it's not funny anymore."

Suzanne didn't like seeing Hank break down. She was used to a guy who seemed so in control, so quiet, a thinker. Even though he was fascinated by death in an abstract manner, the possibility of anyone really dying was altogether different.

"Hank, we all feel helpless. That's why it's a good idea for us to be out here looking. At least we're doing something, not just sitting in the lodge wondering what's going on. Where did you go last night?" If Suzanne could get him to talk, get him to concentrate on the moment, he'd be all right.

Hank didn't cooperate, just took off walking, setting a fast pace.

Clouds continued to drift in until there was a pewter ceiling over the forest. Fingers of fog lifted off the lake and reached for them as they walked the shoreline. A predictable rumble of thunder constantly moved closer to them.

Bringing up the rear, Kathleen slipped on wet pine needles and her feet slid out from under her. "Oh, great." She rubbed her ankle.

Suzanne and Tamara stood and turned to help her. "Are you all right?" Tamara asked. She bent to look at Kathleen's foot.

86

"Look!" Hank shouted. "Up there, beside those spruce." He took off running.

"What is it?" Suzanne froze in place, torn between running after him and helping Kathleen. She grabbed Kathleen by one arm, Tamara lifted the other, and they pulled Kathleen up.

"I'm okay; go ahead. I'll catch up with you. I can't run."

"We're not leaving you behind." Suzanne took charge. "We're all going to stay together, no matter what. Hank knew that."

"He was chasing someone, I think. He'll be back in a minute." Tamara kept Kathleen moving.

"Can you keep walking, Kathleen?" Suzanne asked. "Did you sprain your ankle?"

"No, just twisted it. I think I can walk it off. I'll be fine in a minute. Let's sit down."

"You'll get stiff. I vote we keep moving, even slowly. You can lean on us if you need to." Suzanne gave Kathleen more support on her right side while she limped along.

They didn't make much progress, and there was no sign of Hank. It was obvious that Kathleen's ankle was worse than she was saying.

"I think we'd better go back to the lodge before we get too far away." Tamara made that decision, but Suzanne had to agree with her. She wanted to keep going, but she knew that Kathleen couldn't walk much farther.

"What are we going to do if we find people, anyway? We may be walking right into a trap. We don't have any plan, any weapons." Tamara sounded discouraged.

"How can we make a plan? But if we can trust your feelings and everyone is all right, we need to get them out of wherever they're locked up. They must be locked up or they'd come back—don't you agree with that?"

"I trust my feelings. I've never felt such fear." Tamara acted as if they doubted her now.

"I didn't say we don't believe you. I just said—"

"We can't start to fight with each other." Kathleen interrupted Suzanne. "I've got to rest again."

"Your ankle is swelling badly, Kathleen," Tamara pointed out when Kathleen collapsed on a tree stump and stuck out her leg. "We should take your shoe off, but we wouldn't get it back on. We aren't far from the lodge now. I'm going to get an Ace bandage from the first-aid kit." Tamara took off.

"Tamara! Don't leave us. Don't be stupid!" Suzanne couldn't stop Tamara without running after her. That would mean leaving Kathleen alone. She stood, torn between the two. Then she kicked a pine cone and started pacing back and forth, back and forth along the path.

"She'll be all right." Kathleen rubbed her leg. "I hope."

It was only a few seconds until they heard the voice. It was deep, distorted. And coming from the fog, now thickening around them like cool, icy cotton candy, its direction was muffled. At first it seemed to come from in front of them, then it was behind—now right, now left.

"Kathleen, Kathleen," the hoarse whisper wavered. "How do you like it so far?"

"Tamara, is that you?" Suzanne yelled into the whiteness.

"First-rate performance, huh?"

"Hank?" Suzanne tried again. "Don't be silly. We're not scared."

"Kathleen, Kathleen. Quite a scene, quite a scene."

"Who are you?" Kathleen said in a loud voice, visibly shaken, but her voice was strong. "Why are you doing this?"

There was no way to tell if the voice was male or female. It had a strident note, but was still pitched in a low register.

"The ghost of Macbeth. Hank believes in me now. He's ready to watch. Are you ready, Kathleen? You've hated me all along; you haven't believed in me. Are you ready to believe?"

"Stop it!" Suzanne shouted. "Go away. Leave us alone."

"Yes, I will now, but I'll be back for you. Soon."

Suzanne stood, staring into the dim woods, then finally realized she was holding her breath. "Is it gone? Who was it? Did you recognize the voice?"

Kathleen shook her head back and forth, unable to speak, it seemed. "Why, why?" she said finally. Placing her head in her hands she began to cry softly.

Tamara stepped out of the fog, startling Suzanne. "Tamara, did you hear it? It wasn't you, was it? Please say it wasn't you." Suzanne didn't want to think it was, but Tamara had just left them. She knew exactly where they were. Had she tried to frighten them?

"Hear what? What's wrong?" She bent to take off Kathleen's shoe and wrap her ankle with the Ace bandage she'd brought from the lodge. "I didn't see anyone or hear anyone. I didn't hear anything. This fog is like a sound barrier. It's giving me the creeps worse than anything else that's happened. I just want to claw it away. I feel like I'm surrounded by cobwebs, being suffocated by them." Tamara's eyes were wild and she tore at her tangled hair.

"Hey, Tamara." Kathleen took both of Tamara's hands in hers. "Calm down, calm down. You're all right. We're still here with you."

Suzanne looked at her friend, her head bent, leaning on Kathleen's knee. Doubts flooded in on her like the fog, suffocating her with a growing suspicion. She didn't know Tamara that well. They hadn't been to each other's homes. All she knew about her was what Tamara had told her. They'd been together at school a lot, and Tamara was friendly; but come to think of it, no one else seemed to be Tamara's friend.

Maybe Tamara had pretended she was psychic. Everything she had told them could be an act. They were all good actors and actresses. That's what got them here. Maybe for some reason Tamara was pulling off this crazy stunt. Or maybe she was losing her mind. She thought she had extra powers. She thought she could talk to or hear someone. People did go crazy, no matter what their age.

Sometimes strong feelings made people turn into monsters. The brain was so complicated, the least little thing could go wrong and cause someone to become psychotic, out of control. Suzanne had also read someplace that there was a very thin line between high intelligence and insanity. It was

90

obvious from her grades and things teachers said about her that Tamara was extremely brilliant.

Or maybe Tamara *was* psychic and that had gotten out of hand. She couldn't control it, and it had turned into some kind of obsession or unbalanced reasoning.

You hate me, don't you? the voice had said.

Who was it that thought Kathleen hated him or her? Could Tamara have decided that Kathleen hated her? Suzanne looked at the one friend she had at this new school, and a strong sense of doubt took control of her senses.

CHAPTER 11

Before anyone could say anything else, Tamara dashed off through the fog. She disappeared as quickly as into a deep pool of water. Not even her hand stretched back toward them like the woman's in Friday night's ghost story.

"Tamara, come back. We don't hate you, we don't!" Suzanne yelled.

"You think that was Tamara speaking to us from out of the fog?" Kathleen tried to stand up by herself. Suzanne grabbed her arm to steady her.

"I don't know. I don't want to think it was, but why did she run off again? I don't know anything. I don't know who to trust." Suddenly Suzanne wanted to run, too. To run and run and run, to get away from all this. But they were on an island. Where could she go? She bent double and took several deep breaths.

"Okay now?" Kathleen had her arm around Suzanne, patting her back as she would comfort a little child. "I can walk. Let's go back inside and wait."

"For what? For someone to come and get us? To carry us off someplace, to murder us? Wait for *what?"* Suzanne realized she was screeching, her voice high and shrill like Monica's.

"Wait for the boat, of course. Jay will come with it. I know he will." Kathleen spoke in a calm voice, somehow too calm in light of all that had happened in the last two days. "What time is it?"

Suzanne took another deep breath and glanced at her watch. "Only nine o'clock."

"The fog will lift. It has every morning. The boat is coming back for us at three. We all need to get ready."

"That's a long time, Kathleen." Suzanne ignored Kathleen's saying "all," and started to worry about her teacher. Was she suddenly denying that anything had happened to *most* of the group? "But, yes, let's go back to the lodge and wait. We'll think of something to do."

Every tree seemed to have eyes that followed their progress back through the woods to the lodge. They were performing for an audience of birches and maples, firs and spruce. Pine trees applauded with a rustle of needles against rough bark. A curtain of maples whispered as it pulled back, revealing the soft earthen pathway.

Crazily out of control, Suzanne's mind brought back roles she had played before getting the part of Lady Macbeth, all of them a part of her now. Her first was Little Red Riding Hood. Without meaning to, she looked around for the wolf to come out of the forest. "The better to see you with," the wolf whispered. She peered into the gloom, blinking her eyes quickly, straining to find him, to see him first.

If anything, the fog had gotten thicker. She

could see only inches ahead, two steps, three toward the lodge.

You are late. You are late.

"I am sorry, Mrs. Mortar," said Mary from *The
Children's Hour.* "I went to get you these flowers.
I thought you would like them and I didn't know
it would take so long to pick them."

There are no flowers in these woods, thought
Suzanne, herself again. How strange, unless they
have already died in preparation for winter.

" 'I'm not lying. I'm not lying!' " Suzanne turned
and shouted to the woods. " 'I went out walking and
I saw the flowers and they looked pretty and I didn't
know it was so late.' " She struggled to stop her
mind from drifting like the wisps of fog that seemed
to be squeezing out the lines stored in her brain forever. Her worry, her fear was forcing her to access
them in random order, connect those long-ago
learned speeches to today's situation. " 'I'm not lying. There are no flowers here.' " She gripped both
hands into fists and squeezed them against her chest,
fighting to keep from bursting into tears.

"Flowers?" Kathleen asked. "What are you talking about, Suzanne?" Suzanne's shouting had
brought Kathleen out of her daze. It was as if they
were taking turns with their confusion, backed up
by growing fear.

" 'We must have flowers for their funerals,' "
Suzanne murmured before she could stop herself.
" 'Mounds of flowers.' "

"Flowers would be nice," Kathleen agreed.

"When We Dead Awaken," Suzanne added.

"What?"

"I tried out for the Ibsen play. I was too young."
I'm too young, Suzanne heard over and over in her

94

mind. I'm too young to die. They are too young to die. If I didn't have Kathleen with me, I'd go find them. I'd wake them up. Even if they're dead, I'll wake them up.

She shook her head to clear it. What was happening to her? She had to be responsible. She and Kathleen were the last ones left, and Kathleen seemed to be sleepwalking.

Kathleen leaned heavily on her arm, grasping tightly, fingers closed around Suzanne's wrist like a death grip. "I have always done this. It should have been all right."

"What, Kathleen? What should have been all right?" Suzanne knew what she meant, but she tried to keep Kathleen talking. It would help her. It would help both of them, keep Suzanne's mind from wandering. She was strong. She had to be strong for her and Kathleen.

"I have always taken my kids off before we started a play. It's a part of the process. We needed to bond, to become a whole so rehearsals would go well."

"We are bonding," Suzanne said with some irony. Not knowing what else to tell her teacher, she concentrated on their slow progress. Why was it so quiet? No birds sang from high in the treetops, no loons called from the lake. Even their feet made no sound because the ground was so soggy and the path padded with pine needles.

The lodge loomed up suddenly, dark and forbidding in the cottony setting. But it would be cheery and warm inside.

The big front room was empty. Suzanne expected Tamara to be there. Willed her to be there.

She stirred the fire, blowing it gently back to flames. Then she stacked on a couple more logs.

Kathleen had started to shiver the minute they came inside. Suzanne covered her with a yellow blanket from someone's bed, then started to walk away.

"Don't leave me here alone, Suzanne." Kathleen reached for her. "I think there are just the two of us left. We need to stay together until the boat comes." Kathleen sounded as if she was back in the present, acknowledging but resigned to what had happened and their helplessness.

"Kathleen, I want to look around for Tamara." Suzanne squeezed her hand. "I won't go out of the lodge, and I'll only be gone for five minutes. I promise. Stay right here by the fire. I'll make us some hot tea when I come back."

Suzanne didn't really expect to find Tamara. She just needed to look. The hall was dim with shadows, as if the ghosts of all the people who'd been here over the years were watching her peek into every room.

"Tamara," she called. "Are you here, Tamara?" She walked faster. "Dammit, Tamara, be here. Be here!"

The emptiness magnified the smell of musk and mold. Leftover laughter from Scouts and church campers mocked her as she searched. Her feet thudded on the grayed rag rug that carpeted the hall. New, it had been blue and lavender and burgundy, someone's idea of colors that would stand the test of grimy tennis shoes and muddy boots.

Her room was empty, of course. But Suzanne's eye easily caught the scrap of heavy, cream-colored paper on her bunk. She recognized it im-

96

mediately. It had been torn from Hank's journal.
Her hand shook as she held and read it.

> *Harbinger, don't bother trying to clean*
> *from you the blood*
> *of what you do*
> *Anymore—we all know the loon . . .*
> *You kill with a song,*
> *A Western Union tune,*
> *That delivers a grave pronouncement.*
> *Portend . . . portend . . .*
> *It makes a difference messenger boy—*
> *You only sing the thing . . .*
> *It's Death that has written the song*
> *And yet another*
> *That accompanies with an instrument.*

The loon—the loon, who only announces death.
Hank had written this poem during the weekend,
she knew. When? When had he thought of it? Before people started to disappear? After? After he
made them disappear? Had Hank left the poem for
her to read? To frighten her? Was he laughing
now, along with the loon, imagining her reading
it?

She stared at Tamara's bunk, wanting her to
smile and say, Yes, I read it. And I just needed a
few minutes alone. Let's go back to Kathleen.

A sudden quickening of her pulse made Suzanne
need to get back to Kathleen herself. She turned and
ran, the thump, thump, thump of her steps echoing
behind her.

"Kathleen, Tamara isn't here," she said as she
turned into the living room.

The cheery fire crackled and popped. Orange

and red flames licked the new log, feeding on it hungrily.

But Suzanne felt that nothing would cheer her up ever again. The fuzzy blanket she'd pulled over Kathleen spilled across the floor like an opened cocoon. But no butterfly fluttered around the room.

Kathleen was gone.

CHAPTER 12

Suzanne's first reaction to being all alone was to run, to run and hide in some closet and stay there until someone from the boat came searching for them.

Why her? Why was she the last one left? Was it coincidence? The others were easier to take—kidnap—kill? She didn't even know which word to use. Was it because someone knew she was afraid of being alone?

She flopped on the couch in front of the fire and pulled the blanket around her. She was cold, so cold. Staring into the flames, she mulled over the alternate to her question. Was it design, a plan, for her to be the only one left of their group who didn't know what was happening?

Once more she toyed with the idea that this was some kind of initiation. She was the new kid on the block, new to the theater group. Were they all acting out some bizarre game, a theater game planned by Kathleen? Kathleen had waited until next to last so she could study Suzanne's reaction to each disappearance? This was a test? Of what?

She couldn't think of any possible reason for Kathleen to spend the weekend playing tricks on her. An hour maybe, even a couple of hours, but they were supposed to be working on the play. Kathleen had brought a film version of *Macbeth*. She had the craft materials for masks, and some costumes. They all had scripts. Plenty of work to do, to fill the time, instead of filling it with a huge prank.

No, if this weekend was planned, it wasn't Kathleen's doing.

Suzanne spent some time thinking about each individual who had come to the island. She didn't really know any of them well, but she was searching for any clue that might point to one of them as having initiated this series of disappearances. Again, for what reason? Well, skip the reason— she didn't have to know why, just who.

Again and again, her mind settled on Hank. Him with his obsession with death. Just last week she'd read a news article about a teenage boy who had killed a child because he was bored. His teachers had all said he was very intelligent. Everyone who knew him was surprised by his action. He'd said he was interested in what it would feel like to murder. Hank was fascinated by death. Could he want to find out what each person's reaction might be to his or her own death?

If she settled on that, she'd have to think that all her friends were dead. She couldn't believe it. But if they weren't, then someone was hiding them someplace.

As she warmed her body, anger flamed inside of her. It started in her stomach and spread up and down her body until it pushed her into action. She wasn't just going to sit here and shiver, wonder, speculate about what was going on. If people were hiding from her or being hidden on this island, she was going to find them.

She felt better making a decision about what to do. Grabbing her jacket, she let herself out the front door. She'd explore quietly at first. She'd stop and listen. Surely she'd hear anyone else moving around. She was no wimp. Except for Hank, and possibly Sol, she felt she could fight off anyone who attacked her.

How about the caretaker? Where was he? His son? She didn't know, but somehow she didn't think they were involved in this scheme. The situation had something to do with their play group.

Consciously, she made the decision to start looking away from the lake where they had come in. She didn't think she could stand hearing the loon's cry right now. Some sunlight was filtering through the trees, creating rays with celestial ambience. Heavenly spotlights searching for someone who deserved to be featured in today's drama.

There was no choice. She was the only player. Wasn't she? A bird melody floated down the beam of light, then another. She must be alone. Birds stopped singing when there was danger, didn't they? Danger to them, not to her, unless they had a mutual enemy.

Her feet were on a path. She hadn't chosen it. It had chosen her. The path led to the stables, where all was quiet. One by one the horses looked up at her, then continued pulling at hay and chewing with contented unconcern. Nothing seemed amiss to them. And they weren't having to work. They couldn't ask for more. She thought of riding one. She could cover the island faster. She wouldn't feel so alone.

No, she could move silently by herself.

It took her about fifteen minutes, walking as fast as she could and still being quiet, to come to the other end of the island. It was about a mile long, then—not that great a distance.

Instead of following the shoreline back, she picked another trail, one through the heart of the island, the one on which all the buildings sat waiting for her.

The first was another lodge. It should have been locked, but the door stood open a few inches. Had the caretaker or Andy unlocked it earlier and forgotten to close it? She stood in the doorway, waiting, listening, straining her ears for any tiny sound. Then she tiptoed inside.

She hurried from room to room, feeling as if someone were watching her. There was an energy about the lodge, leftover vitality from all the campers who'd stomped through here in sneakers and thongs and hiking boots. But no one, none of her friends was inside the place. You didn't look in closets or under beds, a voice whispered inside her head. "And I'm not going to," she said aloud.

Practically running, she left the building and fled down the path. Several cabins crouched in the growing light. The fog was lifting at last. Systematically she approached each, footsteps padded by pine needles. Instead of going inside, she peered in through dirty windows, cobwebs clinging to corners, a summer's dust coating the panes, clouding them over, but not keeping her from being able to see in. No one was visible.

She came to the cabins which bordered the big lodge they'd used this weekend. Some were almost dormitory size. Those she went into. All were unlocked. Maybe Mr. Russell never locked anything over the winter. There was probably no reason to. Maybe the cabins didn't even have locks, just hooks or clasps on the doors.

In the biggest room, after she'd peered into all the corners, she felt a presence near her, practically overhead, behind her. Slowly, carefully ready, she turned. Brown eyes questioned her being there. Oh, god, it was a squirrel, a stupid squirrel. It sat on a top bunk like a small brown teapot, stiff with apprehension itself.

"Get out of here!" She stomped her foot, releasing her breath, her fright. Then she hurried outside and downhill.

The caretaker's house stood just as they'd left it yesterday. The door was open. Inside, the radio was smashed. She bit her lip and looked into the bedrooms, feeling she was trespassing. The place was too personal. But no one was here.

Andy's room had posters like any young teen's would display. One with an interest in movies, she corrected her thinking. Horror movies. Was that why he'd liked the ghost story? He was a reader. There was a shelf of Stephen King books, Dean Koontz, early horror writers like Le Fanu and Poe. Andy might not say anything, but he wasn't dumb if he could read these. The vampires and monsters and murderers depicted on the posters did nothing to help her mood. She left, shaking off the creepy chill playing over her spine.

It was outside the house that she first heard the voice. At first she thought she was imagining it. She spun around, but saw no one, nothing. She strained her ears to make out the words.

"Come. Come to me, Suzanne."

"Who is it?" Spinning around now, she shouted. "Who's there?"

It was the loon who answered. The long eerie wail drifted through the trees, tapped into her mind, then faded back to the water.

Laughter followed, not that different from the loon's cry. It surrounded her so that she couldn't tell the direction of the voice.

Her hands began to sweat; perspiration trickled down the inside of her arms. She hugged herself, turning, turning in place, peering into the shimmery light.

A dry limb snapped behind her. She spun around. No one. A soft thud, a crackling of leaves that escaped the rain because of thick foliage overhead. Something or someone was stalking her.

She followed the sound with her eyes searching, her body slowly rotating. Almost afraid to blink, she stared.

"Suzanne, come," the voice called. "You're all alone. You don't like to be alone, remember. Come to me."

She couldn't tell if the speaker was male or female, but it knew her. It knew her name. It wasn't some monster or beast that stalked. She could handle its being a person. And it was one of the play cast. No one else had heard her confess that she was afraid to be alone. Hank? Tamara?

Some of the anger she'd felt returned. "Who's out there. Show yourself. You're a coward, aren't you? You're just trying to scare me, and you're not doing it. I won't let you scare me. Where are you? Where are my friends?"

"Here. Heeerrrre. Follow me. Come. Come with me, with meeee." The voice drifted away.

And despite a little voice inside her that said, No, don't do it, Suzanne, don't go with it, she followed.

Stepping off the path, tracking the soft footfalls, the fading call, biting back the bitter taste of fear, she obeyed.

CHAPTER 13

It was easy to follow, since the person ahead of her crashed through the underbrush. The snapping of branches, the swish of low limbs said here, here I am. Follow, follow, this way, this way.

The voice deep inside her continued to suggest caution—slow down, wait, hold back, follow carefully. The part of her that disobeyed was so needy, craved company so badly, that it overruled caution. She needed to know there was at least one other person in the world. She wanted to stop living the nightmare that probably everyone at some time has experienced: that fear of a holocaust or natural disaster that left only her alive on the earth. For all of time mankind has banded together so as not to experience the awe of the universe alone. The world was too big for only one person. There was a dim, atavistic memory inside of her that haunted her. She wandered the earth searching, searching for a companion, one other survivor.

But surely this person who had survived the weekend's experience was the one who had caused her friends to disappear. She was the last and now it wanted her.

This was the thought that finally stopped her.

106

She ducked behind a clump of willows and crouched low, breathing hard, sucking air deep into her lungs and letting it out quietly. If it would come back for her, if she could see who, or what, it was, then she could decide whether or not to follow.

By hiding she might be able to lure it back so she could follow without its knowing.

The forest was denser here. Wilder. She was not at all sure what poison ivy looked like. Vines twisted around the trees as if to squeeze life from them. Tendrils reached out for her and tangled in her hair as she crawled under them.

The ground was dryer under the shelter of the vine-hung bower. She huddled into as tiny a ball as she could get, giving herself time to think, to regain her composure. She had to stop calling whoever had spoken to her "it." That gave the person a nightmarish quality that was too frightening. Male or female—choose. Male. *He* wanted to lure her to a place where he could easily attack her. Add her to his collection of—of bodies. She wasn't able to stop that word from entering her mind. *Captives*—that was better. It suggested that her friends were alive and being held hostage.

A branch snapping whipped her head around. She was just in time to see a black-cloaked figure disappearing into the woods below her hiding place. He had come back for her. He was no longer calling to her, but now looking quietly.

On hands and knees she slipped out of the bushes, careful not to make a sound. She straightened and hurried after the shadow, slipping downhill ahead of her.

There was a security in following him, instead

107

of his following her. Had he followed her for a time before he called out to her? It didn't matter, and she didn't want to think about it. She was in control now, she convinced herself.

They were heading for the lake, but away from the dock where they had come in Friday night. He had disturbed the loons. There was a splashing and then a chorus of their trembling calls. The sounds chilled her and brought her to a stop. She took the clear notes as a warning.

There were old trees here, off the trail. The trunks were large enough to hide behind. She would wait him out. He'd come back for her. She was sure of it. She was the last one. Whoever he was, he wanted them all.

She still had no knowledge of why he had saved her for the last. The situation seemed planned. He could have taken her earlier as easily as any of the others.

The why of it continued to tease her mind, but no answer came. Until she knew who he was, there could be no speculation on her part as to why he had done this.

As she had predicted, the black-robed figure returned. The cloak and the hood, which she recognized from the costume box, the one Willis had been wearing earlier, shaded his face enough to keep her from seeing who he was. But one thing was for sure now, it was one of them. One of the cast.

She held her breath, hardly blinking, hoping for a clue to the person's identity. Was it Hank? Had his highly intelligent mind twisted out of shape? Had it stayed obsessed with death long enough to want to experience it, cause it, watch it happen?

Turning, he seemed to fade away again into the woods. She followed silently, with even less fear now. If she could confront him, reason with him—

An old building, perhaps a boat house, abandoned for the newer one near the dock, crouched near the lake. He rounded the corner and seemed to disappear inside. Hope filled her. Perhaps everyone was tied up inside. If she could get him out and her in, she could untie them, get some help.

She would play his game. Evergreens cluttered the hill, slid down the slope, leaning backward. They huddled close to the weathered walls of the structure. Choosing a cluster of three, she stepped behind them and called out softly. "I'm here. Come outside. Come and get me."

She pitched her voice in a stage whisper, but loudly enough to carry across the water, to surround the old building. He couldn't help but hear it.

"I know you're in there. Come, come to me."

She started to shake. Her voice would give away her fear if she spoke again. So she waited.

He waited.

Rays of sunshine bounced off the lake, now nearly free of fog. It was going to be a lovely, warm day. Three loons sailed past the boat house, looking like wind-up toys since their paddling feet weren't visible.

She waited.

He waited.

Should she call out again? Was he counting on her to make the first move? Was this a battle of wills, with her not knowing her opponent?

She lost. Suddenly she could wait no longer.

Was he even in there? Had he gone inside, or had he crept past the door and back around into the woods?

Quickly she looked behind her. No one. She listened, ears straining for the least sound. There was the slightest ripple of water against the shore. Rich loamy smells filled her nostrils. A deep breath filled her lungs with pine scents. Her mouth was dry and cottony. Swallowing was difficult.

Windows on the building were low. If she could see inside, she might be able to decide what to do next? Looking back again, she stepped out. One, two, three steps, listen. Nothing. No one. One, two, three, four. Her own feet made no sound.

A few more steps took her to the window. It was covered with dirt and cobwebs. Smearing it with her fist, she peered inside the gloomy interior. For a second she thought she saw a light flicker, like a candle flame or a flashlight beam flicked over the window.

She glanced over her shoulder, then moved around the side toward the front of the house. Wouldn't the caretaker have looked here? Wouldn't Andy have known about this building, checked it earlier? One last tree stood beside the building. She stepped behind it so she could watch the door.

Her body tensed, expecting someone to reveal himself at any moment. She was being foolish. He could be watching her and laughing, laughing and waiting. She glanced over her shoulder, then back.

The front of the boat house was in full sunlight now. Anyone could see her from the woods. But the door faced the water so she could keep watch easily, too. An old dock, boards rotting and crumbling, ran from the lake almost to the door. The place was no longer used.

She had come this far. She walked five steps, reached for the doorknob, clung to its brassy cold metal. Turning it slowly, she pushed gently. The door swung easily, not even creaking.

Coming from the sunny outside, she blinked rapidly, trying to get her eyes to adjust to the gloomy interior. A picture started to emerge from the dimness. A picture she tried to comprehend, tried to deny as soon as it came clear.

The stage was set in a way to distract her just long enough. He stepped from the shadows behind the door, raised his arm. There wasn't even time to ward off the blow. A curtain of darkness fell over her conscious mind as she crumpled to the floor.

CHAPTER 14

When Suzanne came to her senses, an over-whelming panic surged through her body. She struggled, trapped and helpless, against the ropes that held her prisoner, tied to a chair. All she could do was stare with horror. The scene had been set by a master of lighting. Candle flames flickered from around the room.

In the dimness the audience, consisting of four persons, hunched in a row. Windows in the boat house were small, so not much light entered, making the interior fairly dark. When her eyes adjusted, she saw Kathleen, Lucille Stubblefield, Clyde Wilkins, and the caretaker, Mr. Russell, seated in chairs along one wall. Each was tied securely to his or her chair, and rags were tied across their mouths to gag them.

Kathleen's eyes were wide with fear and disbelief, but Suzanne was relieved to see that she was alive. Miss Stubblefield appeared to be asleep or unconscious. Suzanne preferred to believe that than the alternative. Clyde Wilkins groaned and mumbled, but his eyes were closed. Mr. Russell's eyes blazed with anger at his helplessness. She could see that he was straining against the ropes, not believing he couldn't get loose.

On a makeshift stage drawn with chalk lines a production of *Macbeth* was under way.

Monica was dressed as Lady Macbeth, but she played all the parts, since the rest of the cast was incapable of speaking.

" 'Is this a dagger which I see before me?' " she asked, quoting Macbeth's lines, " 'The handle toward my hand?' " In her hand she held a wicked-looking weapon. The handle was black with red jewels set into the ebony. The blade, thin and curved slightly, dripped with liquid crimson.

Suzanne's heart pounded and her eyes flew from person to person to see if any showed a knife wound. Across the front of Sol's white shirt a scarlet stain spread like a fully opened rose. His head was tipped forward so that his chin rested almost at the top of the stain.

She whimpered, thinking the worst. Monica had stabbed him and now spoke his part reverently.

" ' Art thou but a dagger of the mind, a false creation, proceeding from the heat-oppressed brain?' " Monica bent and showed Sol the blade, as if asking the question of him.

It had not been a man following her in the woods, calling to her, but Monica. Monica was out of her mind, Suzanne knew, and she shivered uncontrollably. At the same time she struggled with the ropes around her hands. She must get loose. Was Sol dead? She ached to go to him, to touch him. How many others were in the same condition?

Monica leaped into Lady Macbeth's lines, which Suzanne already knew by heart. " 'That which

113

hath made them drunk hath made me bold; what hath quench'd them hath given me fire. Hark! Peace!' " She swung around and laughed her demonical laugh. " 'I have drugg'd their possets, that death and nature do contend about them. Whether they live or die.' " Her laughter echoed around the large, open room. "Live or die, live or die," she repeated. "It's my choice, isn't it, you players? I choose whether you live or die."

Suzanne's eyes flew from person to person again. Each was made up carefully, but the makeup, rather than being the conservative style which served the play, was garish with a nightmarish quality.

Monica's face was powered almost white. Her lips were a slash of crimson which turned down on each side, turning her mocking mouth into an evil bearer of the words that told the tale.

At the edge of the stage, chalked off to contain the play, sat three witches, hair teased wildly. On June's head rested a black paper witch's hat, fashioned like those children might make for Halloween. Her glassy eyes, made even wider by a line of black eye pencil, stared at the net of spiders draped over the hat and surrounding her face. From where Suzanne sat it was impossible to say whether or not the spiders were real or black plastic imitations. But she feared the wild look on June's face was not an imitation of death.

Biting her lips, Suzanne squeezed back the tears that pooled in her eyes and spilled over onto her cheeks. June had been Monica's only real friend, and this was how Monica had rewarded that friendship.

Bitsy's hair—no, the wig,—was the wildest tangle of all, and full of wisps of grass and twigs. Fastened behind one ear was a cluster of yellow leaves, and pinned to the dark green sheet which fashioned her costume were other leaves—maroon and red and orange. Someone had dressed her with infinitive care. Her face was streaked with white makeup, smudged with black, giving the effect of age—sunken cheeks, lines under eyes, wrinkles finely drawn in where wrinkles would someday be on Bitsy's face. Her eyes were closed. Suzanne prayed that she was drugged or unconscious, but not dead.

It was impossible to assess Tamara's condition. In an attempt to have her standing, Monica had tossed a rope around one of the beams in the ceiling of the boat house. She had fashioned a harness that fit around Tamara's chest, holding her upright. But Tamara's chin rested on her ragged costume's neckline, and Suzanne couldn't see her face. An old broom was tied into her hand, and the handle leaned on the wooden box which was supposed to be the witches' cauldron.

Skipping ahead—Monica seemed to have no need to recite the play in any order—or maybe she didn't know the lines in order, she continued. " 'Double, double toil and trouble; fire burn and cauldron bubble.' " She danced wildly around the three witches and their pot. " 'O, Well done! I commend your pains; and every one shall share in the gains.' " Tossing her head back she cackled as she continued to quote lines. " 'Well done! my witches, well done!' "

If she lived to ever again hear the loon's call, Suzanne would always remember Monica's laughter, this maniacal scene of her dancing around the

115

three girls playing witches for this production that Monica had so carefully staged.

Two players balanced the stage, and Suzanne knew they had to be Willis and Andy. She recognized Willis's funky tennis shoes, and the slight build of Andy. There was no way to tell what condition they were in, however, since their faces were covered by masks. One of them was Kathleen's, splotchy with purple and gray paint, suggesting bruises and sunken, dead skin. The other was a grinning skull, eyes dark sockets, mouth silvery white rows of perfect teeth.

Two, there should be three. Hank! Where was Hank!

All the while she had been forced to watch, Suzanne struggled to scrape and tug off the bandanna that gagged her. When she was finally successful, she confronted Monica, unmindful of how it might spoil Monica's performance.

"Monica, listen to me, listen," she pleaded. "Come to your senses and let me go. Let everyone go while we can help those who need help. You don't want to do this."

" 'I have done no harm,' " Monica said. It was Lady Macduff's denial speech. " 'Whither should I fly? I have done no harm. But I remember now I am in this earthly world, where to do harm is often laudable, to do good sometime accounted dangerous folly.' "

Should Suzanne try to reason with Monica or join her delusion that she was starring in her own production?

When Monica started into a ritual of washing her hands, trying to erase the blood, Sol's blood, which now actually stained her hands, Suzanne

116

searched her mind for words that might catch Monica's attention.

" 'Here's the smell of the blood still: all the perfumes of Arabia will not sweeten this little hand. Oh, oh, oh!' " On her knees exactly at center stage, Monica held both hands to the ceiling, the dagger clutched between them, pointing down.

" 'What's done cannot be undone,' Monica," Suzanne picked up on a later line of Lady Macbeth's. "Lay the dagger down, Monica. Place it on the floor. 'To bed, to bed, to bed.' " She paused, hoping the lines were reaching Monica. Was she totally mad, or was there some reason left, some of Monica left, to hear Suzanne's voice? To care what happened next?

"Lie down, Monica, lie down. Sleep, sleep. You cannot undo what you have done, but you can forget it now and sleep."

"I cannot sleep. I have the part," Monica whispered. "I have it now. It is mine. The lead is mine, all mine. I am the star. That cannot be undone. All eyes are on me. It is mine, I am the star."

"Yes, Monica," Suzanne cajoled. "You have the lead. You are Lady Macbeth. You are playing it beautifully. We are all watching you. We applaud your performance."

There must be some of Monica left. She remembered she wanted this part. In some way, she remembered the disappointment that had pushed her into this new play she had written and carried out over the weekend.

"You have staged this play beautifully, Monica. The costumes are perfect. The lighting is especially effective." Candles flickered, casting the shadows which danced off the silvery gray walls of the old boat house. "But the curtain is coming down. The play is over. Your audience needs to leave. Let them go home, Monica. They'll come another day to see you again."

Desperately, Suzanne searched her mind for what to say to Monica. This might be the only chance she had to get away from her, to save those around the room who were still alive. One wrong word might send Monica into a frenzy of anger and madness. She still held the knife. She had used it on Sol. She could use it again and again if she felt compelled to do so.

"The play is not over. I don't want it to be over."

"Okay. Okay. Keep playing it. We're watching, Monica. The audience is with you. Keep speaking."

Monica stared at the ceiling as if trying to remember what lines came next. She stared out into the audience, her eyes resting on Kathleen as if she expected the director to prompt her.

"I can't remember my lines," she murmured.

"Yes, yes, you can." Suzanne said, her voice calm and soothing. "Yes, of course you can. Start back to where you do remember."

The kneeling figure collapsed for a moment, huddled close to the floor. Then she straightened and raised the dagger again.

"Confusion." She paused. "Ambition, 'thriftless ambition.' "

"Yes, go on." Say anything, Suzanne begged silently. Any words that come to you, any line from the play will do, just keep talking while I think.

Suzanne had tugged at the ropes that bound her

hands behind her until her wrists were raw. Now she wiggled them more, ignoring the pain.

" 'I must become a borrower of the night, for a dark hour or twain.' " Monica paused. "I was the best. I've always been the best. Can't you see that? No one knows that but me. Why does no one see that I'm the best at all the parts? I am always perfect. She expects me to be perfect."

"Who?" Suzanne picked up on this last remark. "Who expects you to be perfect, Monica?"

"My mother, of course. I have to be perfect for her. I always have. She only loves me when I'm perfect. And I'm my father's little girl. He loves me. I know he loves me like a woman, but I can't tell anyone about that, especially Mother. I can't tell Mother. I was perfect today, wasn't I? I will never be perfect again. So Mother will never love me again. She'll never love me again, will she?"

Suzanne couldn't see Monica's face, but she heard the anguish in her voice. "She loves you, Monica. You were perfect at last. Now she will always love you."

There was something about Monica's speech that left Suzanne afraid to breathe. And when she saw the dagger coming slowly, slowly downward, she guessed at Monica's plan. Her state of mind. If she could never be perfect again for her mother, she would stop her life here.

"Monica, don't, please don't!"

As Suzanne repeated the words over and over, her voice desperately seeking to reach Monica, she felt something just behind her. She felt the warmth of another hand in hers, fingers touching her, trying to get her attention.

CHAPTER 15

Suzanne bit her lip to keep from screaming out. By a process of elimination, she knew the hand that touched her had to be Hank's. He was behind her. And somehow, he had wiggled close enough to help her get loose.

His fingers, which she knew had to be tied as hers were, fumbled with the rope that bit into her wrists.

Monica, changing her plan, got to her feet and continued to recite. Her voice rose higher and higher until she was almost screaming some of her lines. Then she'd drop into a whisper and start over. Pacing back and forth, she performed mainly for the audience of adults she had tied and seated in the "front row" of her theater. As soon as Suzanne stopped talking to her, she seemed to forget anyone was behind her. Her face, shiny with perspiration, took on the pallor of wax. Rouged roses blossomed on each cheek. Her mouth, distorted already by the crimson of the lipstick, twisted and grimaced as she mouthed each word succinctly.

As soon as he had freed Suzanne's wrists, Hank banged his hands on hers to say, now untie me. Quickly she did so, struggling with the first knot,

120

but as soon as the ropes loosened, Hank was able to slip his hands out.

Did he have a plan? Should she? Surely the two of them could overpower Monica and take the knife away from her.

She had felt Hank grasp her hand as if he meant, Wait, I have planned a signal for us both to act. Before Suzanne could signal back, Monica whirled and came toward her. It was all she could do to keep her hands hidden, not to reach out and protect herself.

Unaware of the situation, Monica planned to play cat and mouse with Suzanne. "I've wanted to kill you ever since you came here, Suzanne. Did you know that? You're too much competition."

Suzanne forced her voice to remain calm. "I knew you didn't like me, Monica, but I don't think killing me is going to solve your problems."

Listen to me, Suzanne thought. I sound like the classic shrink, listening and advising my client.

"What if I do it because I'll enjoy it? What if I don't care about solving my problems? No one can solve my problems." Monica waved the dagger back and forth and then held it out between both hands, admiring the blade. "And Hank missed the first death. He will enjoy seeing your reaction to death. Won't you, Hank?"

Monica pointed dramatically at Hank, then swirled around and back, dancing with death. She toyed with her victim, unaware that Suzanne was no longer helpless.

Staying aware of Monica, where she was at every moment, Suzanne tried to judge the best time to attack. Monica had to be very strong to have gotten all the cast here and tied. She would have had to drag the men, especially Mr. Russell, who was a large, muscular man. And Hank had an athlete's body, hard and strong. He must weigh nearly two hundred pounds.

Was he watching and waiting? Were his legs unbound as Suzanne's were? Monica had obviously felt that tying their hands was enough.

"Do you plan to kill all of us, Monica?" Suzanne asked. "One by one? You can't get away with this. You have too many witnesses. Remember your audience."

Monica glanced at Kathleen, tossed back her head, and laughed. Then she swirled away, her cape swinging gracefully around her. She bent over Kathleen, who cringed and stared at her.

"What do you say, Kathleen? You're the director. Shall I kill everyone? Or just a selected few? I'll have to kill everyone, I think. I can't leave any witnesses."

She was not entirely mad. There was an element of reality in her thinking.

"Will you then kill yourself?" Suzanne asked. "If you're the only one left, won't it be obvious that you're the murderer?"

"I can always say I escaped. I can be very convincing. You're forgetting what a good actress I am. You think you're the only one who can play a lead role, don't you?"

Monica shrugged off her cape and in her long white dress glided back across the floor, arm raised, dagger pointing toward Suzanne. "This is not my first lead, you know. I had many before you came on the scene."

"What other roles have you played?" Suzanne

122

planned to distract Monica. She still waited for the best time to make her move.

"Are you playing for time, Suzanne? I am not dumb, you know. See, Hank. First she tries to outsmart me, distract me. Maybe she thinks I'll forget my plan."

"You do have a plan, then?" Suzanne felt Hank's touch again. Was he saying it was time?

"Not entirely. I have always enjoyed improvising, being spontaneous. 'I am the master of my fate ... the captain of my soul,'" she quoted, swirling away again, then back. "To let Suzanne be or not to be," she misquoted. Then the laughter. Tossing her head back, she cackled, her voice rising and falling with merriment. "Not to be, I decide." She made her decision, and came at Suzanne, dagger raised, her face a mask of pure desire and pleasure.

"Now!" Hank jumped up, shoving his chair back with a bang.

Suzanne leaped up a split second later, but Hank pushed her aside as Monica brought the dagger down toward her chest.

Hank was unable to keep Monica from plunging the knife into his own arm as he grabbed her wrist a second too late.

Recovering her balance, Suzanne grabbed Monica's outstretched left arm and swung her to the floor. Quickly she stepped on the hand that still held the dripping dagger, causing Monica to have to release it. Immediately, Suzanne kicked it toward a dim corner of the shed.

Monica was in no mood to give up. She rolled over and grabbed Suzanne's ankle, causing her to fall hard. Pain exploded through Suzanne's knee as she came down on it, unable to catch herself in time. Ignoring the fiery ache in her leg, she scrambled across the splintery floor and tried to stand. Before she could get to her feet, Suzanne felt Monica tackle her, knocking her flat again.

In a death grip, Monica wrapped both arms around Suzanne's legs. She was screaming wildly. "No, no, no, you won't escape me. I must punish you, I must. You were my prisoner."

Hank wrenched Monica off Suzanne. "Can you get up, Suzanne? Find the rope that tied our hands. Quickly. I'm having a hard time holding her."

Monica had the strength that came with desperation. She twisted and tugged and pulled. Before she could escape, though, Suzanne kicked Monica's legs as hard as she could. She fell again, face forward, and Hank was able to twist her arms behind her. Quickly Suzanne wrapped the cord around and over, under and around, then knotted it securely.

It was obvious they had to tie Monica's ankles as well. Running back to her chair, Suzanne picked up the other piece of rope. She wrapped it around Monica's kicking feet, finally getting them together and tight.

Suzanne had never seen such a look of pure hatred as that on Monica's face. "You won't forget me." Monica delivered the line, punching out each word, giving each equal importance. "This is not finished."

"I think it is, Monica." Hank stood and stared down at their prisoner for a few seconds.

"You're hurt." Suzanne pulled off the bandanna that had covered her mouth. She tied it tightly around Hank's arm to stop the blood that flowed freely down over his hands. Hank raised both hands and looked at them, one clean, one slippery, dripping crimson drops across the floor in a random pattern.

"We are all forever wounded," he said, his deep voice carrying, echoing off the boat shed walls. The words were melodramatic, but they made a fitting last line. The curtain should fall. They should all hug each other and laugh and call out congratulations. Then they should take hands and prepare to bow.

But the audience was quiet, so quiet. There was no thunder of applause. No bravos! No whistles and shouts.

And the star sobbed with frustration and anger.

Suzanne felt a lump of anguish start in her chest and rise, threatening to choke her. She pushed back her own sobs and ran to untie the rest of the cast as Hank started on the "audience."

CHAPTER 16

Suzanne ran first to June, fearing the worst. She was right. A finger placed alongside June's neck found no pulse. She was dead. Suzanne found no visible mark on her. But there was a frozen look of terror that told her a lot. Could June have died of fear when Monica draped her with a net of spiders? Some of the spiders were plastic, dime-store variety. But many were real. A large brown leg stretched toward Suzanne's fingers. A hairy wolf spider seemed to stare at her with its multitude of eyes. A black widow, with its shiny round body, crawled toward her.

She shuddered and moved quickly to Tamara. First she loosened the harness and untied Tamara's hands. Tamara groaned as Suzanne lowered her carefully to the floor.

"Tamara, are you all right? Please be all right," Suzanne pleaded. I suspected you, she added to herself. How could I have thought you'd do something like this?

Like this? Suzanne could never have imagined a scene like the one Monica had played out—over the weekend or just now. Had she planned this, or had it come to her gradually? Had she seen the op-

126

portunity to bring June here to the boat house, and then continued one by one as she became obsessed by her vision?

Tamara's eyes fluttered open, full of fear. But when she realized that it was Suzanne holding her, she relaxed and started to sob.

"It's all right, Tamara," Suzanne soothed her. "You'll be all right." Would any of them be all right? She hugged Tamara tightly, then laid her gently on the floor. Curling into a ball, Tamara continued to cry, but softly, no longer hysterical.

Leaving Tamara, Suzanne ran to Sol. There was a faint pulse, but he had lost a lot of blood. If they could get help soon, he might be all right. She untied him. "Help me, Hank. Let's get Sol lying down and cover him."

"Is he alive?" Hank hurried to help her ease Sol to the floor.

"Barely. He's probably in shock. I think he's lost a lot of blood. Bring me Monica's cloak. It's the warmest thing I can see." Suzanne cradled Sol's head in her lap, smoothing back his dark hair from his eyes. She leaned forward and kissed his forehead, willing him to feel her touch, to care, to want to fight and live.

She said a little prayer as she tucked the black cloak around him, making him as comfortable as possible. Reluctantly, she left him.

Bitsy was woozy from whatever Monica had given her,—had Monica kept her doped all this time?—but when Suzanne freed her, she put her head between her legs and struggled to gain her senses. "What happened?" she asked softly.

"You don't want to know right now, Bitsy." Suzanne hugged her. "Just try to clear your head. We need your help."

There was anger in Lucille Stubblefield's voice as she spoke. "Lordy, kids, I thought we were all done for. I don't know how you got loose, but thank God you did." Standing, rubbing her wrists and legs for circulation, Miss Stubblefield helped Hank lower Clyde Wilkins to the floor. "Don't you die on me, Clyde. Don't you dare die. Remember how many times you've asked me to marry you? Well, the answer is yes. I want a Christmas wedding. The sooner the better. Hear me? Don't you try and get out of this. I've waited so long. Oh, Suzanne, have I waited too long? Have I been a foolish old woman?"

"No, of course not, Miss Stubblefield. He wouldn't dare leave you now."

"He's okay, Miss Stubblefield," Hank said. "I think he was drugged."

"He'd better be all right or I'll never forgive him. I've got a lot of plans for him. For us. We're going to retire and have some fun."

Despite the situation, Suzanne felt a smile tug the corners of her mouth upward. Maybe this was just what this couple needed to convince them they wanted to be together formally. Her eyes met Hank's, and they laughed softly.

Taking her elbow, he whispered. "I think we'd better leave them alone now. See about Willis. I'll check on Andy."

When Suzanne took the mask from Willis's face, she cringed. On the side of his head was a swelling covered with dried blood and matted hair. Quickly she felt for a pulse. It was strong and steady. A pungent odor made her wrinkle her nose.

128

She had never smelled chloroform, but if that was what was keeping Willis under, it meant Monica had planned some of this. She wouldn't have accidentally found the drug on the island.

Kathleen approached Suzanne on unsteady legs. She put her arms around Suzanne. "I will never, never take a group away like this again." Kathleen was openly crying.

"Kathleen, this would never, never happen again. This is not your fault. You are not responsible for Monica's state of mind. From what she said, I think her mother and father have contributed to this. From what Monica said and what June said earlier, I suspect that Monica has been abused at home by her father."

"Just that by itself would be a heavy load to carry." Hank put one arm around Kathleen and hugged her close. "Suzanne is right, Kathleen. None of this is your fault. You don't need to feel guilty."

"I will. I will forever." Kathleen sat down again and gripped the back of the chair, her knuckles white. "We shouldn't have tried *Macbeth*. I was the only one who thought we could do it."

"The superstition will continue," Hank said.

"You're full of dramatic lines." Suzanne couldn't resist the remark. "Do poets always talk like that under stress?"

"Score one for you, Lady Macbeth."

"Don't call me that, Hank. I never want to read the play again, and I certainly could never play that role."

"We'll skip the senior play this fall," he said. "But knowing Kathleen, as soon as she comes to terms with this, she'll find something we can handle."

"Poor Monica." Suzanne glanced at the bundle of frothy white dress that was now deathly quiet on the floor.

While they talked, they had untied Andy and his father. Mr. Russell suggested they all get down to the dock. "What time was your boat coming back?"

"About three, I think. If you can help us, Mr. Russell, we'll get people over there. Then Hank and I will pack up everything and bring it down. I don't think Kathleen will be much help."

"What should we do about June?" Hank asked.

"I'll get a sheet from the lodge. Is it all right to move her, or should we leave—leave her here?"

"There will be a radio on the boat. Let's leave her here until we call the police. I'll do it, Suzanne," Hank offered. "You help Kathleen."

"Give me a job, young man," said Lucille. "I'm fine, and Clyde will be soon. He's coming around."

"Help Bitsy, Miss Stubblefield," Suzanne suggested. "I'll stay with Tamara until she can walk."

Hank touched Suzanne's shoulder. "Can we do anything for Sol?"

"I don't think so. I don't know what to do. Maybe we shouldn't move him, either, until we have the boat here." A sob escaped when Suzanne thought about Sol. She took several deep breaths. You can't lose your cool now, she scolded herself. There's too much left to do.

In a move that surprised her, Hank took her in his arms and held her very tight. "You were terrific, Suzanne. I don't want to forget to say that.

130

Hold on for a little longer. Then you deserve a good cry. I may even join you. I think we may all be in shock. When it wears off, we're going to need each other."

"Thanks, Hank." Suzanne let the tears flow unchecked, but when Hank released her, she mopped her face with her sleeve and went to Tamara.

"What's happening, Suzanne?" Tamara mumbled. "My head feels like a basketball and my body aches everywhere."

"It would take too long to tell you now, Tamara. Can you stand up? I'll help you. We need to get to the dock."

It was nearly three o'clock by the time they had all gathered at the boat dock.

Kathleen's husband jumped off the boat as soon as it neared the shore. "Are you all right, Kathy?" He ran to her. "I've tried to call since Saturday night. I guess you had that storm that swept the northern part of the state. Power lines have been down everywhere." Jay looked around. "What happened here?"

"We need to use the boat's radio, Mr. Reed," Hank said. "Kathleen can tell you, but we need some medical help and the police here as fast as possible."

"Try for a helicopter for Sol," Suzanne called to Hank.

Hank came back to her. "I checked on him again, Suzanne. I'm sorry. We won't need it." He took her arm and squeezed it tightly, holding her when her knees threatened to fold under her.

Taking several deep breaths, she bit her lip and tightened her whole body. "I'm all right. Thanks, Hank."

"You sure?"

"I'm fine for right now. We have a lot to do." She looked for someone to help to the boat.

Going home was only the beginning for them. The police would come to the island, there would be a lengthy investigation. They'd all have to tell their stories.

It was Willis, though, regaining his sense of humor, that began their healing. "Remind me guys." He touched the swelling on his head and winced. "I don't ever, ever want to have any fun again."

And the remark that Tamara had made on arrival came back to Suzanne as the heavily loaded power boat swung around and pointed its bow toward the mainland. "You won't need a camera to remember this weekend, Suzanne."

She realized that she hadn't taken one photo the whole time they were on the island. But it was true: her memories might recede, she might be able to tuck them into some dark room in her mind and close the door for a time, but this production was going to haunt her forever. This improvised drama in which Monica McCheever had played the most dramatic role of her life.

As the boat pulled out, a single loon cried, his voice echoing around them. He had opened this drama. It was fitting for him to have the last line.

TERRIFYING TALES OF
SPINE-TINGLING SUSPENSE

THE MAN WHO WAS POE   Avi
71192-3/$3.99 US/$4.99 Can

Is the mysterious stranger really the tormented writer Edgar Allan Poe, looking to use Edmund's plight as the source of a new story—with a tragic ending?

DYING TO KNOW   Jeff Hammer
76143-2/$3.50 US/$4.50 Can

When Diane Delany investigates the death of her sworn enemy, she uncovers many dark secrets and begins to wonder if she can trust anyone—even her boyfriend.

FIELD TRIP   Jeff Hammer
76144-0/$2.99 US/$3.50 Can

On a weekend field trip, Tom Martin doesn't know who to turn to when students start disappearing, leaving behind only their blood-spattered beds.

ALONE IN THE HOUSE   Edmund Plante
76424-5/$3.50 US/$4.50 Can

In the middle of the night Joanne wakes up all alone… almost.

ON THE DEVIL'S COURT   Carl Deuker
70879-5/$3.50 US/$4.50 Can

Desperate for one perfect basketball season, Joe Faust will sacrifice anything for triumph… even his soul.

Spine-tingling Suspense
from Avon Flare

JAY BENNETT

THE EXECUTIONER   79160-9/$2.95 US/3.50 Can

Indirectly responsible for a friend's death, Bruce is consumed by guilt—until someone is out to get *him*.

CHRISTOPHER PIKE

CHAIN LETTER   89968-X/$3.99 US/$4.99 Can

One by one, the chain letter was coming to each of them... demanding dangerous, impossible deeds. None in the group wanted to believe it—until the accidents—and the dying— started happening!

NICOLE DAVIDSON

WINTERKILL   75965-9/$2.95 US/$3.50 Can

Her family's move to rural Vermont proves dangerous for Karen Henderson as she tries to track down the killer of her friend Matt.

CRASH COURSE   75964-0/$3.50 US/$4.25 Can

A secluded cabin on the lake was a perfect place to study... or to die.